Nexum Trend

Selling herself for an education

Ray Oslow
Katie Oslow

Dark Fantasy Press

Contents

Lets get real

Writing this sort of fiction can be challenging. You always worry that people will take your words the wrong way, or fail to understand the difference between a fantasy and a reality.

Outside of writing fiction, we try to advocate for safe, sane, and consensual (SSC) kink as much as we can. We have written (under different pen names) guides on how to participate safely and respectfully in BDSM dynamics. Much of what we write is miles away from what we advocate in the real world.

This story is absolute fantasy, the kind of thing you might imagine in a role play. Sometimes it can be fun for a couple to imagine themselves in a situation like the one depicted here, but when they do, they should always recognize that it is in the act of play. A healthy relationship is a relationship where the humanity and value of every person are respected.

Too often, I have heard horror stories from people new to kink being taken advantage of by predatory people that would use a work of popular fiction, out of context, as justification for their bad behavior.

Always remember, consent is key above all things. All kink involves inherent risk, take precautions to make those activities safer. Risk Aware Consensual

Kink (RACK) should always be practiced. Research any activity before you try it. Research any lifestyle before you dive in. Always make sure everyone involved fully understands and is enthusiastically prepared to participate.

Be Kinky, Be safe
Ray & Katie

Independence

Kimberly stormed down her front lawn dirty blond hair swaying in her wake dragging her suitcase, ignoring her mother's insults. Her brunette friend, Daisy, was behind the wheel of the waiting blue compact car at the curb. Kimberly pulled the door open, "Trunk!" she yelled.

Daisy pressed a button on the dash and the small trunk swung up. Kimberly threw her bag in, turned back to her house and flicked the bird at the closed door before dropping into the passenger seat.

"Just go!" she said, trying to hold back the tears in her eyes.

"Kimmy, whats.." Daisy's voice was cautious.

"GO!" Kimberly growled. Then softened her tone, "Please! Just, just go!"

Daisy pulled away from the curb and navigated out of the neighborhood. With nowhere else to go, she pulled onto the highway and began making her way to the center lane. Traffic flowed past them in silence.

Kimberly looked with blurred vision out the window, despite her efforts, tears were rolling down her cheek. That wasn't the mother she remembered. How could she have changed so much?

Growing up, Kimberly and her mother had been close, sometimes she seemed more like a best friend than a mother. That had all started to change in the past year.

Kimberly's dad had suggested they try a new church. None of them were excessively religious but they tried to get into the pews a few times a month. After the family had attended a service at this new church, Kimberly's mother had hit it off with a few of the women and the world began to shift.

At first Kimberly's mom just started doing a better job of getting them to church on Sundays. Then she started going to meetings and talking constantly with the woman's group. Before long, she was chiding Kimberly for wearing outfits the two of them had bought together and insisting Kimberly pray with her for a chaste and holy husband.

Kimberly's dad was no help. To him, keeping his daughter out of trouble was a good thing. He did start spending more time away. Then, at Christmas the two had "The Fight". Kimberly still wasn't sure what had started it, but her daddy had stormed out to end it and wasn't living with them anymore.

After that, life got harder for Kimberly. Her mother insisted she wear only dresses, and every one of them was some hideous thing with floral prints and skirts that almost reached the ground. Kimberly had worn her normal outfits under the dresses and would pull the ugly frock off in April's car on the way to school every day, until her mother caught sight of her in the background of a photo in the parent newsletter. Kimberly's mom had gone through her room and confiscated all her "sinful clothing" leaving nothing but the most conservative dresses behind. It was a devastating moment for her and she would have said it destroyed her social life if she still had one. Senior parties and dances were forbidden, and she was able to see her friends less and less.

Now, with graduation on the horizon, Kimberly's mother had dropped the biggest bomb.

Her mother informed her that, because women only go to college to find husbands, and that there were plenty of good and holy boys at her church, she would not pay for Kimberly's tuition as they had planned since she was in grade school.

The money in her college fund would be withdrawn at a significant tax disadvantage and donated to the Church because the Pastor had said that he needed the money to do God's work.

Kimberly had frantically called her father for help but he sounded defeated, saying "Your mother has control of the accounts sweetie. I can't do anything about it, sorry."

She tried to plead with him to intervene on her behalf but her father wouldn't even talk to the woman. In the end, she cursed the coward and hung up in time to see her mother glaring at her in the doorway.

That's when the fight got worse. After a fiery back and forth Kimberly's mother said, "If you are so hell-bent on being a harlot in the world, you can get out of this house!"

"Fine!" Kimberly shouted. "And I'll fuck every boy I see along the way you CUNT!" as she slammed the door to her room, texted April to come get her and pulled her suitcase from under her bed. She stood for a while staring at the collection of dresses in her closet then back at the empty case. She hated every piece of cloth in front of her. Delaying the decision, she gathered up what makeup she still had stashed away in hiding places in her room, as well as her underwear and threw it in the bag.

There was a knock at her door. Wondering if her mother wanted to make peace, she opened the door with high hopes.

They were dashed immediately. A pile of garbage bags filled with clothing were piled in front of the door.

"There's your whore clothes! Leave the proper outfits, I'll give them to a decent Christian girl!" her mother called as she disappeared down the hall.

Both enraged at her mother's cold insult and relieved to have her clothes back, she gathered up the bags and filled her case with her essentials.

At last, she pulled the paisley dress she wore off and threw it on the floor, pulling on a denim miniskirt and backless halter top with no bra to support her C cup breasts. Her nipples were quite apparent through the sheer silky cloth. One last parting shot for her mom.

When April pulled up, she grabbed her case and started down the stairs.

"I'm not paying for that phone anymore either, young lady!" her mother called.

Kimberly pulled her phone out of her pocket and just dropped it on the hardwood steps, watching it tumble down the stairs to land with a cracked screen at the bottom. She was sure to drop her case on it when she reached the foot of the stairs and was gratified to see the rainbow distortions on the screen around the cracks.

Her mother began a string of invectives and Kimberly was out the door.

Now the two girls were rolling down the highway in silence.

"She threw me out," Kimberly finally said.

"For real?" April asked in disbelief. "You sure this isn't just a fight?"

"Pretty sure." Kimberly replied.

April shook her head. "She'll come around. Graduation is next week. She'll call you back and apologize in no time."

"She took my phone," Kimberly said. "Well... she said I couldn't keep it so I smashed it."

"Oh shit!" April said, not knowing what else to say. "You want me to take you to your dad's."

"Fuck him too!" Kimberly snapped.

"Oh." April sighed.

They drove aimlessly, April not knowing what to do with her friend, for over an hour as Kimberly cried, then raged against her parents and then cried again. Finally she asked, "Are there any... uh parties?"

"Huh?" April asked.

Kimberly looked at her friend. "Parties, graduation and all that. I've missed so much. Let's just go get drunk, get fucked and forget for a while!"

"Kimmy, you're a virgin!" April chided her.

Kimberly turned to look out the window, 'Tell my mom that! If she thinks I'm such a slut, I may as well get started!"

"I don't like this Kimmy!" April said. "Let's just head over to the Dinner and get some pie. We can figure out what's next from there."

"Fine," Kimberly said.

The Dinner was one of the few places high school kids could hang out without being hassled. As a result, the parking lot was full of cars Kimberly and April recognized from the school parking lot. As they walked in, they spotted Shauna and Lisa sitting at a round corner booth. Each had a stack of papers open in front of them. Lisa saw them and waved them over.

"What's shakin?" Lisa asked as they came up. "Kimmy, looks like you got your wardrobe back! Congrats!"

Shauna looked up and her eyes went wide. "Mrs. Masters let you out like that?"

"Yeah," Kimberly said as she slid into the booth next to Shauna. "For the last time!" She pulled a french fry off Shauna's plate. "I may be well dressed, but I'm officially homeless!" She popped the fry into her mouth while quietly wondering how she would eat and where she would sleep now.

"No shit!" Lisa exclaimed. "The bitch threw you out?"

"Yep," Kimberly replied.

"So where are you gonna go?" Lisa asked.

"No fucking clue." Kimberly said glumly. She realized how hungry she was and pointed at the plate.

"I'm done," Shauna said.

Kimberly pulled the plate in front of her and took a bite of the half club sandwich that remained. She thought about it and realized that she had never tried a club sandwich before and that they were not her favorite. Still with the sudden reality of not knowing where her next meal would come from lingering over her head, she resolved to finish every bite.

"What about State?" Lisa asked. You were all excited about their history program?

"No college, no college money!" she said. She set the sandwich down. "The fucking scammer of a pastor gets my fund."

"Oh crap!" Lisa exclaimed.

"Her mom even took her phone!" April chimed in.

"What the fuck?" Shauna shook her head sympathetically. "What are you going to do?"

"Get a job I guess." Kimberly sighed. "No chance it will be enough to pay for school though."

"Financial aid?" Lisa asked.

"Parents make too much, we already looked into it." Kimberly replied.

"Yeah but, they kicked you out." Lisa argued.

"Won't matter." Kimberly said.

"Loans?" April asked.

Kimberly shook her head, "I could try I guess, don't know how that's going to work with no one to co-sign. Never looked into it cause I had 'the fund.'"

"Fuuuuuuuck," April said sympathetically.

"Well," Shauna ventured. "There is one other option." She flipped the pages in front of her back to the first one and pushed it over to Kimberly. It read

Private Nexum Contract

Application for service

90 day tier

Kimberly read the title several times. She looked up at Shauna in disbelief, then over at Lisa who apparently had an identical document in front of her. She looked back down at the pages and flipped through them. There were limits checklists, listings for weight and measurements, a bunch of legalese and on the last page, Shauna had signed under "Applicant".

"You're going to be a Nexum girl?" Kimberly asked in shock.

"If I can match!" Shauna said. "Lisa and I are both applying for the summer, a lot of girls are doing it. We should finish our contracts just as the college kids are moving into campus. We're gonna spend a gap year in Europe and come back to school next fall. This will pay for all of it and then some."

"Yeah, but," Kimberly didn't know how to put this.

"Your going to be sex slaves!" April cut in, her voice shocked.

"Nexum girls," Lisa corrected her. "Slaves are forced to serve. Nexum girls can quit anytime they want and still get paid for the time they work."

"Splitting hairs!" April argued. "Everyone knows you give up a huge bonus if you quit early! They even call the guys who buy the contracts 'owners'!"

"Oh Jesus!" Lisa exclaimed. "The feminist is here."

"Kimmy!" April turned to her friend. "Don't even think of it! You're a virgin! The stories I have heard…"

"Are all just sensationalism!" Lisa argued. "Sex work is legal now and Nexum Contracts are a hell of a lot safer than working the streets! One guy with a rule book! I bet Kimmy could make enough to fund her entire education in one summer."

"Virgins get a bonus!" Shauna piped in.

"Disgusting!" April exclaimed. "Come on, Kimmy, let's just head back to my place. You can sleep over and we can figure out something tomorrow!"

Kimberly was no longer paying attention to the conversation. She was reading through the explanation of responsibilities and contemplating the limits list. Finally, she looked up at Shauna. "Can you get me in touch with this lawyer?"

"Kimmy NO!" April exclaimed. "Don't you want your first time to…"

"Be with my husband?!" Kimberly cut April off. "Like my mother demands? Or be for love, or to mean something? BULLSHIT!" Kimberly flipped to the limits sheet, there was a $ amount next to every checkbox. "Look at this, I leave enough of these unchecked and…”

“…and you get abused for 3 straight months!” April snapped.

“…And I'm all paid through my masters!” Kimberly retorted. “After the last year don't you think I can take 3 months of paid abuse? My mother's been doing it for free!”

“Not like this! You're a virgin, you don't know.” April was dead serious now. Shauna and Lisa had grown still. “This whole Nexum trend may sound good, but you jump on this bandwagon and you have no idea what's going to happen.”

“What's going to happen,” Kimberly said confidently. “Is that unlike most girls, I'll get something worthwhile in exchange for my virginity. I'll get my education and with that, I'll get a career and be set for life. I'll Never have to see my mother again!” She closed the document and pushed it back over to Shauna. “Plus, I get to see the look on that bitch's face when I tell her how I paid for it all!”

Negotiation

Kimberly and Shauna sat in antique wingback chairs as they waited for their appointment with Mr. Darrow. The polished wood coffee table held a selection of sailing and financial magazines. Nothing to attract the attention of two 18 year old girls. Kimberly was wishing she hadn't been so intent on pissing off her mother as she packed last week. All she had under her robe for graduation this morning and for this meeting with the lawyer was a white blouse that exposed her belly over a black bra, and a black skater skirt who's hem was 6" above her knee.

"Considering what you're meeting him for, I think it's ideal," Shauna had said when Kimberly climbed into her car after the graduation ceremony. While Kimberly had been staying at April's all week, her best friend had refused to take any part of her plan, so she had decided to tag along with Shauna when she went in for her "sale."

"Shauna Martin?" Called the receptionist from across the room.

Shauna stood up, "Come on," she said to Kimberly who followed her into Mr. Darrows office.

The office was large and lined with bookcases except

the wall to the right where a bay window looked out over the James river. The building had once been a historic mansion and Mr. Darrow worked hard to preserve the aesthetic.

The girls crossed the open floor with its oriental rug and sat down in the two leather seats across from Mr. Darrow.

Darrow was a balding man with round glasses that had dark black frames. The effect made him look like a mole. He stood and smiled at the ladies as they came in and did not sit again until they were seated.

"Good afternoon Shauna, I presume you have finished the application?" he asked while looking Kimberly over.

"Yes sir!" Shauna said and passed the paperwork over to him.

Darrow took the papers and began leafing through them. After a few minutes he let out a slight grunt. "You have checked off quite a few limits here."

"Well, I didn't want things to get too crazy," Shauna said. "I just need enough for a trip to Europe."

"Yes, well...." he grunted again and turned to his computer. "I had already uploaded your measurements and images to the match-maker and there has been interest."

"That's great!" Shauna said. Kimberly noticed that she sounded more nervous than enthused.

"Only..." Darrow was clicking away with his mouse. "With your limits, it cuts out most...no...yes... all of the men who matched you."

"Oh," Shauna said.

"If you could relax your stance on a few items we may be better able to place you," he said. "There are a couple here who are excluded by only one or two of your limits."

Shauna leaned forward and swallowed hard. "One or two?" she took a deep breath, "which ones?"

Darrow smiled without looking away from the screen. "Diapering and ageplay would land you a lucrative contract immediately."

"Oh FUCK NO!" Shauna sat back like she was shocked.

"Yes," Darrow agreed, "That buyer has been very difficult to match. I had to try."

Kimberly sat up and asked, "Are you some kind of used car salesman?"

"Kimmy!" Shauna started.

"No! It's ok Ms. Jennings," Darrow held up a hand. "I'm sorry I didn't catch your name."

"Kimberly, Kimberly Masters," she stared the lawyer directly in the eye.

Darrow smiled. "Yes, Miss Masters, part of what I do IS sales!"

Shauna sat back at the man's admission.

Darrow continued, "Nexum is very new. Did you know that I wrote the first Nexum contract ever created?" He paused but continued when neither girl responded. "As a new business, the market is not evenly distributed. To put it crudely, there is too much of one kind of product," he motioned toward Shauna. "And too many buyers looking for the more, uh, diverse product."

Kimberly nodded. "So you need us to be more open to…. diverse buyers?"

"Just so." Darrow smiled. "And by 'us' am I to understand that you wish to establish a Nexum contract as well?"

"Yes sir," Kimberly replied.

Darrow reached into his desk and produced a stack of paperwork. He handed it to Kimberly saying, "Why don't you get started while I finish with your friend Miss Jennings here."

Kimberly slid forward in her chair and began reading over the contract.

Shauna cleared her throat, "Uh what diversifications do you think would get me placed?"

Darrow turned his attention back to the screen, "Impact and Bondage would open the most doors for you."

Unlike Shauna's Europe trip, Kimberly needed a much larger amount. Keeping this in mind, she turned the page to the "limits" list. As she read them over she winced at some but left them open, she made sure to cross off Diapering and Ageplay, not wanting to deal with Mr. Darrow's problem customer. There were a whole host of biologically disgusting activities that she absolutely had to cross off. There were other terms she didn't recognize, Shauna and Darrow were still busy and she had no phone to look them up, so she left them blank and just hoped for the best. She liked animals so "puppy, kitty, pony, hucow and bunny play" shouldn't be too bad. She also made sure to cross off body modification. She was doing this for a few months to finance her future, she had no intention of carrying tattooed reminders of it for the rest of her life.

As she finished the form Darrow had turned his screen so Shauna could see the headshots of her potential buyers. One was a bald man who seemed a bit overweight, the next had gray hair and a beard while the third had a thick red beard and blazing blue eyes.

"I like him!" Shauna said pointing at the guy with the red beard.

"Mr. Fuller!" Darrow said. "I'll let him know! If he is ready to receive you, I can have you delivered today!"

"Today?" Shauna gasped.

"Is there a reason to wait?" Darrow asked.

Shauna looked over at Kimberly, "Well, I'm her ride."

Darrow smiled. "Tell you what, let me look at your friend's application, maybe I can place her today as well!"

"My car..." Shauna said.

"We can have it delivered where you like or placed in storage for the duration of your term. For a cost." Darrow said.

Shauna looked cornered for a moment. Kimberly's stomach did a flip as well. This had suddenly become much more real. She was going to be some strange man's live-in mistress tonight.

"Are you ready, Miss?" Darrow turned his attention to Kimberly. His smile was wide but his eyes were narrow like a snake's.

Kimberly took a deep breath and passed over the sheets. She looked over at Shauna and shrugged.

Darrow leafed through them for several minutes. The clock on the mantle ticked loudly. Kimberly crossed her legs and pulled at the hem of her skirt as she waited.

Darrow made a couple subtle noises. "Degradation," he muttered.

Kimberly was unphased. After the things her mother had said to her, what could a man say to her that would be worse? At least he would be paying.

Darrow set the sheet down and turned his screen back so that it was facing him. He began typing.

Shauna and Kimberly exchanged glances but said nothing.

Darrow picked the sheet back up and checked it again. "Glory-hole," he muttered as he typed.

That was one of those terms Kimberly didn't recognize. She assumed it had to do with butt sex. Not something she was enthusiastic about, but it had a nice bonus value on it so she figured she would try.

Darrow finally stopped typing and cleared his throat. Kimberly was already looking directly at him.

"Your enthusiasm is very marketable Miss Masters, as is your virginity. It is rare. Typically, an applicant with so few limits, has much more experience." Darrow said. "There are a number of profiles you would fit into!" He smiled. "Many of them are currently online and await only a few images before they place their bids."

"Bids?" Kimberly asked.

"Yes." Darrow replied. "We will narrow the potential buyer pool down with a brief auction. Once it is at a reasonable number, you can choose from the remainder." He picked up a fancy looking camera with a large lens. "If you would just disrobe and step over here where the light is good…"

"Disrobe?" Kimberly sputtered. She pulled at the hem of her skirt again.

Darrow was walking around his desk toward the empty space in the room he had indicated. "Yes, Miss. Given the nature of Nexum contracts, my buyers want to see all of what they are buying. Now please, take off your clothes and step over here. My clients are waiting." Mr. Darrow was starting to sound annoyed.

Kimberly looked over at Shauna who just nodded. "It's part of the deal," she said.

Kimberly took a deep breath as she stood, kicking off her sandals. She unbuttoned her blouse and set it on the chair, then unzipped the side of her skirt, allowing it to fall to the floor.

She looked over at Mr Darrow who just said, "All of it please."

Kimberly unfastened her bra but hesitated. She turned her back to Mr. Darrow as she slid it down her arms and dropped it onto her blouse. She looked over her shoulder to see that the man was watching her. No sign of chivalry at all. She swallowed hard, slid her hands under the sides of her panties and pushed them down her hips. She stepped out of them and, with an arm across her nipples and a hand covering her bush, she moved to the place Mr. Darrow had indicated.

Darrow looked into his camera and then back at her. "You are going to have to lose that modesty real soon," he said in a frustrated tone. "These men aren't buying you to be their bridge partner!"

Kimberly squeezed her eyes shut. Talking about this at dinner last week when she was still seeing red from her fight with her mother was entirely different than now, naked, in front of a pervy lawyer with a camera. She uncovered her C cup tits and moved her hand away from her neatly trimmed mound. She stood there unsure what to do with her hands.

Darrow sighed. He walked over to his desk and pulled out a laminated card. He carried it over to Kimberly and handed it to her. On the card was a sequence of pictures of a naked blond woman in various poses. Under each pose was a name like "Inspection" or "Nadu," across the top was printed in white letters, "Basic Slave Positions," Kimberly looked up at Darrow puzzled.

"We will take a series of shots. You will adopt each position and I will send the picture to the buyers." he said. "Using the slave positions should enhance your sale price. It shows that you know how to submit."

"But I don't," Kimberly argued.

"Girl!" Darrow exclaimed. "Every man waiting for these pictures wants NOTHING more than to teach you how to submit!"

Kimberly was confused. "But you just said that knowing..."

"Attention!" Darrow barked, cutting her off.

Kimberly looked at the card. It was the first one. She stood straight with her hands at her side.

"Drop the card for the picture!" Darrow said.

Shauna giggled.

"You did this?" Kimberly asked.

"No, I just did a couple of poses," Shauna replied.

"Your friend had limits on posture training and strict protocols," Darrow explained. "Since you are open to them, we are getting a full set." He lined up the camera again. "Now drop the card and stand at Attention."

Kimberly dropped the card.

Over the next few minutes, Mr. Darrow had Kimberly walk through five standing positions, four kneeling positions and three positions on all fours. Some, like "ready to please" left no illusion as to what use the position would be put to. Kimberly's cheeks were red and her pulse pounding as she stood up from her last pose that had her face down on the floor, knees folded under her, hands stretched out and crossed in front of her on the carpet, "Humble," the card had read.

She started putting her clothes back on as Mr. Darrow returned to his desk.

"Bids are already rolling in and a few have dropped

out already!" He announced as he sat.

Kimberly was pulling her skirt back up.

"You sure you only want to do 90 days?" Darrow asked. "Couple years at these rates and you would be set for life!"

"Just the summer!" Kimberly insisted. "I need to be done by the start of the fall semester!"

Darrow shook his head. "If you say so."

Kimberly got her top buttoned and sat back down. She and Shauna held hands and Kimberly was a little relieved to feel the sweat on Shauna's palm. It was good to know that she wasn't the only one who was nervous.

Darrow announced every time a bidder dropped out over the next few minutes. Finally, he had the selection down to 3.

"First of all, this is very impressive for a 3 month term! He said. At a base rate of $45 an hour, you are looking at $97,000 if you go full term."

Kimberly's eyes went wide. This was better than she hoped, almost her whole fund restored!

"But..." Darrow continued.

Kimberly squeezed Shauna's hand, waiting for the shoe to drop.

"Each of these men have selected some difficult to match activities." He grinned, "Because they are not popular with our talent, you will be offered a completion bonus if you finish all 90 days of your contract without early termination."

"Early termination?" Kimberly asked.

Darrow smiled, "Well, yes. Despite what the

protestors say, we are not selling you into slavery. You are free to leave any time you like. Just understand that, if you do, you will sacrifice your completion bonus."

Kimberly scrunched her eyebrows. "How much is the bonus?"

"For these kinks?" Darrow smiled. "100% of base rate!"

"HOLY SHIT!" Shauna exclaimed. "Mine is only 50% and I took Bondage!"

Darrow smiled. "Your friend is far more adventurous and that pays well!"

"$200,000 for three month's work," Kimberly was stunned.

Darrow punched some numbers. "Actually it's $194,400 for three months USE," he emphasized the last word in a way that made Kimberly uncomfortable. "If you plan to use that for education, I can have it set up so that you will not be taxed on any of those funds you spend on tuition, room, board, books or fees. All part of the service, no extra charge," he said.

"Ok," Kimberly was elated. This would be more than enough for all four years and maybe some grad school! "Let's see them!"

He turned the screen to show their profiles.

The first was a handsome man who looked to only be a few years older than Kimberly. She was excited until she saw his location. She had no intention of disappearing to Idaho.

The second was an older looking man with white

hair and a white beard wearing a cardigan. He lived only a few miles out of town. The idea of her first time being with a man old enough to be her grandpa gave her a shiver.

The third man was young in comparison. He looked to be in his early 30s, clean-shaven with a square jaw. There was a barn and several horses in the background of the picture. Scanning down, she saw that he was only a couple of hours west of the city. Her heart pounding, she pointed at him.

"Mr. David Zorn." Darrow stated. "I'll tell him to expect you this evening."

Arrival

Mr. Zorn lived on a massive property in southwest Virginia. Mr. Darrow's driver turned the black sedan off the country road, through an arched iron gate and onto a tree lined one lane drive up to the house. On either side of the lane, wide green fields were enclosed by white wooden fences. Kimberly could see several horses grazing in the evening light.

She carried nothing. After her birth control injection, Mr. Darrow stated that her clothes and necessities would be provided by Mr. Zorn and that everything else, including her purse with her ID would be safe with him. She brought up her suitcase and signed a property waiver before she left. Now Kimberly sat fidgeting in the back seat with only the clothes she wore while the 2 story home grew in the front windshield.

The blue house was surrounded on all 4 sides by a wrap around porch and had a red metal roof. Everything looked freshly painted and the bushes around the foundation were trimmed into perfect cubes.

The drive turned into a loop in front of the house with a side line that went to the barn and the garage to the right of the house. The driver pulled around and put Kimberly's door facing the house where Mr. Zorn was rising from a rocking chair on the porch.

Before Kimberly could open the door, Mr. Zorn was down the steps and pulling it open.

"Kimberly Masters? I'm David Zorn." he held out his hand.

Kimberly took his hand and was surprised by his strength as he half pulled her out of the car.

"Uh, hello sir!" she said.

David smiled. "Sir…" he nodded. "Good start." He closed the door and patted the top of the car. The sedan pulled away and was just a pair of fading tail lights in the failing light of the late May evening.

"Come inside Kimmy, we will talk a bit about my expectations before you get started." David motioned with his whole hand up the stairs.

Kimberly felt a little nervous entering this strange man's home. It was silly, she knew. Technically, this man owned her body for the next 90 days. What danger awaited her in that house that she didn't already sign off on.

She climbed the steps ahead of him and waited while he opened the door. Once she was inside, he pushed the door shut and locked it using a key which he showed her before he pocketed it.

"For the next 90 days, you will not go out of this house without my permission." He explained matter of factly as he continued across the open living room into the wood-finished kitchen with gray granite counters.

Kimberly blinked in shock for a moment and then

followed the man.

"Tea?" he asked.

The polite offer seemed out of place and caught Kimberly off guard. "Uh... yes please..sir." she said.

"Sir again. Good for now, though not necessary for long." he said as he poured the steaming tea from a kettle into a cup. He pushed the cup across the counter as well as a bowl of sugar and a small creamer of milk.

Kimberly looked down at the cup, there was a spoon on the counter resting on a napkin. Also on the counter was a small black garment in a sealed plastic bag as well as a dog's shock collar. Her stomach did a little summersault.

She scooped 4 spoonfuls of sugar into her tea and stirred it.

As she sipped her tea, Mr. Zorn motioned to the kitchen table. Kimberly sat down. He walked around to her side of the counter and leaned against it.

"Mr. Darrow is very efficient," he explained. "I didn't initially expect him to deliver you tonight and I can assume you didn't expect to be here tonight."

"No, Sir." she said. "This afternoon I thought I was just going in to find out about Nexum."

"I see." Mr. Zorn sighed. "Well, are you having second thoughts?"

Kimberly hesitated. She didn't expect this courtesy from a man who bought a sex slave over the internet. "Uhh."

"Your hesitancy says it all," Zorn said. "Today was

a whirlwind, and now you are in a strange man's house expecting to be ravished at any moment."

Kimberly finally detected a trace of an accent in David's speech. It was hardly there but a few words came across odd.

David picked up the collar and the bagged garment and placed them on the table in front of her.

"Take a night, in the guest room, alone, to think about it. I'll ask nothing of you until morning." He turned back into the kitchen and retrieved a can of beer from the refrigerator while Kimberly looked at the items. The bag had a label on the front, it was a crotchless bodystocking.

David dropped into the seat next to Kimberly. "If you decide to go, no harm. I'll pay you from the time you left Mr. Darrow's office until the time you return at our negotiated rate. A few hundred dollars is more than enough for the peace of mind that you are going into this willingly."

"Thank you, Sir," Kimberly said. Her eyes were locked on the collar. "Going into what exactly though?" she asked.

David sat back and sipped his beer. "If you stay, you will be my FuckPet," he lifted the collar on one finger. "You will be disciplined quickly for any rule breaking. Leave the property, this administers a shock! If I press a button, it will administer a shock! If you enter an area of the house I haven't allowed you to be in, it will administer a shock. It's tied into the home network and I can access it from anywhere."

"Oh…" Kimberly's mouth hung open as she looked at the collar.

"It is painful, but will do no lasting harm." David assured her. "Once you put it on, only I may take it off you. If you remove it, I will consider it a termination of our contract."

Kimberly nodded, "I understand."

"Your uniform is simple. You wear what I tell you to wear or you wear nothing at all. If I have not instructed you on an outfit for the day, you will spend the day naked. Become used to nudity, it will be your default. To ease you in, I ask that you wear this tomorrow." He put the collar down and tapped the bag. "I didn't know your sizes, so other outfits will arrive in the next few days."

Kimberly didn't know what to say. "Uh, thank you, Sir." she said. Why was she thanking him, he just said she would be naked for the next three months? But he was buying her outfits, so the part of her that learned manners said thank you, despite knowing that whatever he bought would be just as slutty and humiliating as the crotchless bodystocking on the table.

"In addition to the collar, once they are delivered, you will wear wrist and ankle cuffs at all times unless your costume prevents it. Once again, removal will be considered termination."

She nodded and bit her lip.

"You will be leashed. You will be required to remain where I tell you. If you unhook either end of your leash without permission, I will consider it a termination."

Kimberly nodded again.

"That is your default expectation. When I am making use of you, you can expect stricter protocols. I enjoy binding, so you may spend a lot of time immobilized. If I feel you deserve punishment, you will be spanked, paddled or whipped. If I have guests, you will provide them with pleasure as I instruct. This is NOT a monogamous contract."

Kimberly's heart was racing. Visions of being passed around in a gang-bang were marching through her mind.

"You will have other assigned duties such as cleaning," he said. "I also expect a blowjob while I have my breakfast."

Kimberly winced, "I, uh… I've never…"

"You will learn." David sounded reassuring. "I also recognize that you are a virgin."

Kimberly looked down, "Yes Sir."

David nodded. "Well, that is special. We will have to make sure our first time is memorable."

"Thank you," Kimberly said almost in a whisper.

"If you are willing to accept these terms and others like it that I may impose as we move forward, you will be wearing this outfit and your collar when you come down to perform your first morning duty at 8 tomorrow. If you are in your street clothes, I will say nothing in protest, I will just send for a car."

"Yes Sir," Kimberly said, staring at the bag and the collar.

"The guest room is at the top of the stairs to the

right."

Kimberly looked over her shoulder at the staircase, then turned back to Mr. Zorn. He was giving her one more chance. She knew that if she went upstairs now, she could chicken out. Come down in the morning and forget about the whole thing. The freedom that he offered scared her. She needed the money, this was the only way! She blinked and saw her mother's scowl in her mind's eye. She could hear her calling her a whore. If she went upstairs right now, that voice would hound her all night and she would give up. Kimberly took a deep breath.

"Sir?" she asked.

David had been about to get up. He turned, squinting saying nothing.

"Sir, wouldn't you like some pleasure now?" She slid down off her chair and onto her knees in front of him. She rested her hands on his thighs. "Even if I leave in the morning, you are paying for me tonight," she said.

"I am..." David said, leaning back as he looked down at her.

Kimberly tried to do her best pout as she licked her lips. "So you should get some value for your money." She slid her hands up his thighs and began pulling his black leather belt open. "Besides, Sir." She continued as she opened the belt and began on the button to his fly. "How am I going to decide if I want to suck your dick for the next three months......" she had the fly open, he was hard and pressing against his boxers, she pushed the slit in his shorts open and his cock sprang fully erect in front of her. It was larger than she expected, longer than her hand and so thick that her fingers just barely touched as she wrapped them around its shaft. She looked up at his face to see his satisfied grin at her surprise. She took an intimidated swallow and then finished, "...if I don't know how it tastes."

She opened her lips, and then realized she would have to open even wider as she guided a penis into her mouth for the first time in her life. The taste was salty, like sweat mixed with other flavors she couldn't describe. She ran her tongue over the tip and could sense Mr. Zorn's body shift. She had seen porns before and so she tried to slide her lips down and take more of it into her mouth. It got just to the back of her mouth and she suppressed a gag. She pulled back.

"Easy, easy!" David whispered as he stroked her hair with two hands, pulling it back and out of the way. "Don't try and deep throat on your first try, puppy." He had pulled a rubber band from a dish on the table and was wrapping it around her hair into a ponytail. "Just suck the tip and then lick the shaft."

Kimberly pulled his cock out of her mouth and then ran her lips and tongue down its left side.

"The underside is better," he coached.

She looked up at his face, it was kind and gentle looking. She nodded, lifted his cock with her hand and put her mouth on the base where the shaft met the scrotum. She got some hairs in her mouth and tried to ignore them as she slid up the underside.

"Good puppy! Good girl!" He was saying and stroking her head.

She knew she should feel humiliated but his encouragement made her more comfortable. When she reached the tip, she ran her tongue across it and then went back down the shaft, then back up. She cradled his balls in her left hand and used her right hand to stroke what was not in her mouth. She had given handjobs before to boyfriends in high school, she figured she knew what she was doing there. She moved back up to the tip and took it back into her mouth while she began a gentle massaging tugging on his shaft.

"Yes puppy! Thats a good girl!" His voice was less measured. She could hear his enjoyment.   She looked up, with his cock in her mouth and saw that he had his head back. She licked the tip, rolling her tongue all around it. Then back down the shaft, back up, back in. She could taste drops of precum. It was not her favorite! Bitter and salty at the same time but she could manage. Back down the shaft, back up, back in her mouth, pull and tug, and down and up and in and down and....

He clenched his hands into fists and she felt his cock twitch. She was down at the base of his cock, she had a moment to wonder if she should move back to the head when she felt the warm fluid splatter across her cheek. She rushed back up, the next pulse almost caught her in the eye but she clenched it shut in time to feel it across her eyebrow and down her face. She opened wide and pushed it into her mouth.

The pulse filled her mouth with the same foul taste she had already sampled but now it was thicker and seemed to coat her tongue and everything else. The next pulse shot past her tongue and hit the back of her throat. She fought back the gag and closed her lips tighter. The following pulses were less powerful, just dribbling more cum onto her waiting tongue.

She looked up at him and he was letting out a contented sigh. "Ohhh good puppy!" he said. He brushed her hair back and scratched behind her left ear. She slurped as she pulled her mouth off his cock, cleaning it off along the way. She had a mouthful of cum. It was not the most disgusting thing she could imagine but she didn't enjoy it. She looked around, but there was nowhere she could easily spit it out. She grimaced as she looked up at him and swallowed hard. The taste lingered and she tried to make more saliva to wash it out. She looked at the table, the teacup was still there. She moved back to her chair and climbed back up into it and took a sip, swished it around and then swallowed again. It was a little better.

She looked across the table and saw a cute holder with a stack of paper napkins, she took one and tried to wipe her face. To her surprise, the paper tore and stuck a little and she had to press harder than she expected to get it off. Even after wiping her face, she could feel a tightness in the skin where it had landed. She was sure it was in her hair too.

David was looking at her in appreciation with a sly

grin on his face. "Was that a decision or just your sense of market value for the night to think about it?" he asked.

Kimberly took a long slow sip of the last of her tea while she thought about the question. She looked for her mother's voice in her head. After all, she had just given a man a blowjob for money. She was now a real whore. The doubt was gone though. She had done it. She had just made herself a whore in this kitchen! She still had the taste in her mouth. She was a whore. The only question left was, what kind of whore she would be. She looked at the table as she made her choice. She set the tea down.

"Thank you for the tea." she said before she reached across the table and picked up the collar. She wrapped it around her neck tightly enough that she could feel the cold steel of the shock probes pressing against her throat, "My Master." She finished before sliding back off the chair and onto her knees adopting the Nadu pose she had learned in the photoshoot earlier in the day.

"Good Puppy," David said.

Kimberly's first night was spent naked, kneeling at Master Zorn's feet with her head resting on his thigh while he watched an old black and white movie. Occasionally, he would fondle her tits casually with one hand while he watched. Late in the movie, David's penis was hard again. Kimberly missed the conclusion as she was busy giving the second blowjob of her life while the story was settled.

Once the film was over and Master David's balls were

empty, he clipped a chain leash to her collar and led her to the guest room.

"Your bed will be delivered tomorrow, Puppy," he said. "Tonight you get to sleep in here."

He unhooked her leash and then wrapped his massive arm around her tilting her head up and kissing her on the mouth.

His kiss was firm and confident, his tongue pushed into her mouth as though he was demonstrating his ownership of the space. While he kissed her, she felt his hand on her bare belly, slide down into her bush. His ring finger slid across her clit and she stiffened. He pressed it gently and she raised up on her toes. He began to stroke it and her eyes opened wide. He pushed her back and pinned her to the wall. His finger now working her rhythmically, he slid down a little, her knees were weak. She grabbed his shoulders and dug her nails in. He rubbed harder, she had never felt this before. Heat was growing in her, his finger slid down and was just teasing against her opening. She knew that all he needed to do was push in and she would be able to release and.....

He stepped back. "Tomorrow night, if you stay, I will take your virginity."

She looked up at him, she had been so close. "Now... we can now..." she gasped.

He shook his head. "I said we must make it special." He turned his back on her and went into the hall while he pulled his phone from his pocket.

Kimberly felt a sudden stinging pinch in her neck, it made her muscles tense up and she fell to her knees!

The shock collar was excruciating!

"You forgot to say SIR, Puppy!" David said without turning around as he went into his room and closed the door.

First Day

At 8am, Kimberly was in the bodystocking kneeling with her legs apart and her eyes downcast in the kitchen feeling extremely exposed as her pussy was the only part of her body not covered by the sheer garment decorated with swirling patterns. He had left no instructions for her hair, but she remembered the night before and tied it back with a ribbon she had found in the guest room. There was an old grandfather clock in the entry and she could hear it clicking away as she waited for David, her owner. She was still in shock at the idea.

Three days ago, she was a high school senior living in a Richmond Suburb. Now she was an owned Nexum Girl somewhere in Bum Fucking Egypt. Just three months and she could go to college and move on with her life. She pictured her acceptance letter, now being held with her ID and other personal documents by Mr. Darrow. He would be putting in the paperwork to have her mail forwarded to his office as well. No chance for her mother to sabotage her plans by withholding key orientation information. All part of his service, he had said, but Kimberly had done the math. Her first few days of service would just cover her legal fees. David may have meant well in letting her leave this morning, but, had she done so, she would be hundreds of dollars in debt.

She heard footsteps coming down the stairs and rolled her shoulders back. She kept her eyes down, doing her best to imitate the pose from the card. She could still remember the taste from the blowjobs the night before, but she was committed to getting this done. She only hoped that whatever breakfast he gave her would be enough to wash away the flavor.

David came into the kitchen. He was barefoot, but wearing black running shorts and a gray t-shirt with a sports logo on it. He stopped in front of Kimberly. "Can you cook, puppy?" he asked.

Kimberly nodded, "Yes, Sir." Over the past few months, Kimberly's mother had started forcing her to learn all the "skills a good homemaker will need."

"Good!" He walked past her and sat at the table. "Bacon, eggs, toast, and black coffee!" He picked up a tablet and began reading.

Kimberly climbed to her feet and got started. The stove was gas and much nicer than the electric range she had at home. The refrigerator was very well stocked and she found everything she needed quickly.

David used an old-style drip pot for coffee, so Kimberly got it started before everything else.

"Do you drink coffee, Puppy?" he called to her as she turned the eggs.

"A little Sir!" she replied. "With milk and sugar! Sir." she added.

"I prefer mine black." he said flatly.

Kimberly set the plate of food and his black coffee in front of him soon after. David looked over the food, sampled a forkful of eggs, and then a sip of coffee while she stood and waited. He looked over at her. "This is very good!" He pointed down.

Kimberly knelt on the floor.

"From now on, you will make me breakfast. While I eat, you will please me with your mouth under the table. Unlike last night, I expect you to swallow every drop. Once you have finished that task, you can make yourself breakfast before cleaning this kitchen. I expect you to be finished when I return from my run."

Kimberly nodded before crawling under the table.

This time she only licked his shaft at the beginning, to avoid a spill, she kept the head of his penis in her mouth for most of the blowjob while working with her hand and tongue. By the time his bitter seed was filling her mouth her jaw was throbbing with exhaustion. She made sure to suck him clean before pulling her head back and swallowing.

He almost immediately stood up and pulled his shorts back up, tucking himself back in. "Good Puppy!" he said as he made his way down the hall. By the time Kimberly had crawled back out from under the table, he had put his shoes on and was out the door.

Kimberly was seated at the kitchen table resting while she scrolled through her social feed on the tablet David had left behind. She had made almost the same breakfast for herself and enjoyed the coffee as it washed the taste of David's semen out of her mouth. The dishes were washed, the counters wiped down and the stove cleaned off. It looked as if the kitchen hadn't been used at all.

Kimberly was looking at pictures of her friends and wondering what she should post when she came across an image of Lisa at the pool with a caption that said

Summer plans fell through, another
season guarding at the Courts!

Kimberly wondered if Lisa chickened out, or if she hadn't been willing to do what Mr. Darrow wanted to make a match. Kimberly and Shauna had been at the office for most of the afternoon, waiting for the driver and Lisa had never showed up so Kimberly presumed she didn't go through with it. She touched the heart icon and was about to post something when she heard a door slam.

She looked up to meet David's eyes for a moment and then her neck exploded in pain. She dropped the tablet and reached for the collar, she wanted to cry out but the shock had made her spasm and she couldn't get a sound out.

Then it was over.

"I don't like it!" he growled as he stormed across the room. "Puppies don't play with tablets!"

"I'm sorry, Sir!" she stammered but was cut short when he pressed his finger against her lips.

"Do not speak!" he said. "Off the furniture!"

Her heart was racing, she slid off the chair to her

knees.

"On all fours!" he demanded.

She put her hands down on the floor and lifted up into a crawling position.

"Face on the floor!" he commanded.

He bent her elbows, and then slid her arms forward, it was an imitation of the 'Humble' position from the card Mr. Darrow had shown her. Her ass was up in the air.

<WHACK!>

She rocked forward as his open hand struck her ass. Sting and heat radiated from the spot.

<WHACK><WHACK><WHACK> He seemed to strike the same spot on her right cheek every time. Each blow stinging more and sending pins and needles down her leg and up her back.

"Puppies don't use electronics without permission!"

<WHACK><WHACK><WHACK><WHACK> He struck her left cheek in the same sequence with the same force. Her entire ass was now on fire. Tears were streaming from her eyes. She had never felt so much pain before. She wasn't ready for this.

"Puppies stay off the furniture!"

She heard him walk away and then a jingle as he came back.

<CLICK> He had attached a leash to the ring in her collar and was pulling her back up with it. She rose to a kneeling position.

"You are my FuckPet!" He took a position standing directly above her. He held the leash in his hand with no slack, forcing her to keep her face turned up to him. "While you are here, you will get no more consideration than any other pet!"

Kimberly was in shock. His mood seemed so different than before his run. She was in tears, not because of the pain, but because she didn't understand why he was so angry.

David seemed to sense her confusion. His tone remained stern but lost its edge. "While I was out, I thought about our time together. Since you are staying, I truly do own you now. So, I'm going to make the most of this and use you in a way that no woman would let me before!" He looked down at her. "Does this frighten you?"

Kimberly nodded sheepishly.

"Good," he said. "You can take the collar off and leave any time you like, of course."

She nodded.

"So, if I decide I don't like something, you will have to live with it. No electronics, and no furniture for now! Understand?"

Kimberly nodded again and braved a, "Yes Sir."

"Now, the kitchen looks nice," he said. "Let's get you started in the living room!" He pulled her leash as he walked away. She quickly followed.

Kimberly spent the rest of the morning cleaning and dusting the downstairs rooms under Mr. Zorn's supervision. When he approved, he called her a "Good Puppy" if she made an error and did not complete a task to his satisfaction, she received a firm smack on the ass.

For lunch she made sandwiches. David sat at the

table while Kimberly knelt beside him on the floor and ate there.

In the early afternoon a stack of boxes were delivered.

David clipped Kimberly's leash to a table leg in the dining room while he opened and inspected each one.

As he did so, he tossed a pair of padded wrist cuffs to her without a word.

Kimberly picked them up and figured how to fasten them in place. Each had a thick metal ring on the back.

A few moments later a pair of ankle cuffs landed in front of her. She rocked back onto her sore ass as she brought her feet out from under her to bind them as well, then returned to her kneeling pose.

At last, David had finished opening packages. He went back to a flat box he had opened earlier and set it aside.

That afternoon, he had her clean the upstairs, as thoroughly and with as much oversight as he had applied downstairs. It was in this effort that she first saw the master bedroom. It was large, but not as big as she had expected. A king sized bed with metal posts sat between two windows. On the far side from the bed was a dresser. To the right of the door was the master bathroom and a walk in closet.

While she was scrubbing the mirror in the master bath, David heard a sound downstairs and left her alone for a moment.

When he returned he was holding a giant round

cushion, it was a dog bed. He went to the corner on the far side of his bed and dropped it on the floor. "That's where you sleep, Puppy!" he announced.

Kimberly gave him a disappointed look and his smile shifted. He came into the room and put his hands on her hips, turning her toward him.

"Good puppies want to be close to their masters." he said as he ran his left hand around her back and squeezed her still burning ass. His right hand moved up to cup her left breast and he rolled her nipple between his finger and thumb. "Don't you want to be a good puppy?" he whispered to her.

"Yes, Sir," she whispered back. Both hands tightened their grip.

"Just Sir?" he asked.

"Yes, Master," she tried.

"Good puppy!" he sighed and loosened his grip before kissing her.

He lifted her off her feet and set her on the bathroom counter. As they made out, his right hand slid back down to her crotch and found her clit once more. Again he began to rub firmly and she caught her breath, again he teased at her opening, just to get his finger wet and then returned to her clit once more. She began bucking her hips in anticipation of the climax she knew was about to overtake her and again… he stopped.

"Tonight." he said, then lifted his hand, his ring fingertip was shiny and wet. He put it in his mouth and licked it off. "Tonight" he repeated before turning and walking out of the room once more.

Dinner was on the floor again. This time, David had warmed up a stew he had cooked the day before. He set Kimberly's bowl on the floor with no spoon before starting to eat.

"Master, how?" she began.

"Like a puppy, Fuckpet!" He said without looking at her.

Kimberly took a deep breath and went down onto her elbows. She looked up at her owner one last time, hoping for a reprieve. None came. She lowered her mouth to the bowl and began to use her tongue to move large pieces of stew to where she could pick them up with her lips. While she ate, she felt his hand rest on her ass and move down to her clit where he began to gently tease her again. It lacked the intensity to bring her to climax, but it kept her status as a sexual toy in her mind as she ate from a bowl like a dog. The experience was entirely humiliating and yet a part of her kept hearing David's voice say "Tonight".

Despite the humiliation, she wanted more, she wanted his fingers inside her, wanted HIM inside her, wanted him to stop teasing and take the plunge. After a day of sucking dick and cleaning like a maid, being humiliated, spanked, and shocked, she should be furious and disgusted by Mr. Zorn, but all she wanted was to be helpless underneath him.

She slurped some of the broth into her mouth and pushed her hips back toward his hand.

"Good Puppy," he almost purred and pressed his finger firmly against her clit. "Get nice and wet for me tonight."

After dinner, Kimberly was almost insane with desire. The word "Tonight" is all her mind could fixate on. She was going to lose her virginity "Tonight". She was going to be fucked by the man who owned her "Tonight". She was already a whore, but she would truly become a woman "Tonight."

Her leash was attached to a drawer handle in the kitchen while she washed the dishes. David left her alone with a warning about staying off the furniture, he disappeared into the dining room and then upstairs.

When Kimberly had finished cleaning up, he had not returned. With nothing else to do, she knelt on the kitchen floor and waited.

When David saw her, he smiled. "You're learning! Such a good puppy!" he said. He unclipped the leash from the drawer and gave it a gentle pull. "Cumon girl! It's time!"

Kimberly's heart raced. This was it! She hoped it didn't hurt, so many of her friends said it hurt the first time.

She followed him up the stairs and was surprised when he led her to the guest bedroom where she had slept the night before. On the bed lay a selection of white lingerie. David unhooked her leash, and pulled the ribbon out of her hair, allowing it to fall to her shoulders.

"I said your first time should be special." He gestured to the garments on the bed. "So my puppy gets a special treat to wear tonight."

Kimberly looked down at the bed and back at him. "Thank you Sir!"

He put his hand on her cheek and then grabbed her by the chin, holding her firmly. "Just remember, I choose how gentle or how hard you're fucked for as long as you stay here!"

Kimberly's heart raced. She was shocked that this made her want him even more. She wanted him to make love to her gently, but the idea of being fucked mercilessly was just as exciting. "Yes Sir!" she said through her clenched jaw.

"I will await you in my room, Puppy," he said before he turned and left.

Kimberly began pulling at the bodystocking she started quickly at first. After she got her arms free and it was hanging around her waist she slowed down. This was it, this was her first time. She paused and looked at the outfit on the bed. That was what she would be wearing for her first time having sex with a man. Her thighs already tingled and she wanted to be with him, but she couldn't ignore the voice in her head. After tonight, she would no longer be a virgin.

She took her time getting out of the rest of the stocking.

There was a lace bustier see through dress that she gently pulled on, the fabric seemed so thin, her breasts bulged against the cups which were maybe a size too small. She suspected this was intentional. The ruffle skirt flared from her waist but ended only half way down her hips, leaving her pussy uncovered. She ran her fingers along the hem brushing her mound with the tips. This would be for him tonight, and every night for the rest of the summer. There were thigh high stockings she pulled up, she had never worn garters before so it took some time before they were clipped to dangling fasteners from the dress. There were two armbands with thin tulle ruffles around them that she pulled slowly up to align with the top of the dress.

Besides all this was a white headband with inlaid flowers and a single jewel in the middle. She held it between her two hands and looked at herself in the mirror. She was something between a princess and a porn star with her white frilly dress, exposed crotch and visible nipples through the cloth. She swallowed hard, pushed her hair back and set the band into place.

She moved her hand to cover her crotch and then forced herself not to. She was a Nexum girl! Her pussy was buying her education and her future. She told herself to be proud of it, but this was all so embarrassing and frightening. She forced her arms down to her sides. The leather cuffs were resting against her hands as a reminder of her status.

She pulled the door open and walked down the hall. With each step, the hall seemed longer and her steps got shorter.

The lights in David's bedroom were dim and music was playing. The air smelled different and she saw an incense stick burning on a holder set on his dresser.

David was half sitting on the bed with a lopsided grin when she walked in. She stopped at the door, hardly able to breathe. She was sweating, she could feel the moisture under her headband and her scalp seemed to stretch under tension. She could hear her own heartbeat in the rush of blood through her ears. She felt flush and knew she was blushing.

David took her in with a long slow gaze that crawled up her stocking covered legs to the bands at her thighs, up the garters to her exposed mound, to the thin waist where her skirt came together, lingering on her breasts, up her neck, past her collar and then they locked on her eyes. He looked deep into her eyes and she felt more naked under his gaze here and now than she had all day. Finally, after she felt like they had stared at each other forever, he spoke. "Come to me, Puppy."

Trembling, she crossed to him and he put his hands around her. "Beautiful!" he said and then kissed her. As they kissed, David moved himself around so that Kimberly's back was to the bed, then he led her backwards and lowered her. She was on her back and the room seemed to spin around her. David stood up and put his hands on Kimberly's thighs. He pushed them apart and slid his fingers gently up into her bush. His right thumb slid up her slit and found her clitorus immediately. Kimberly started to moan as he rubbed.

He moved his left hand beside and applied pressure with both hands, opening the lips of her labia. He made eye contact with her and then looked down.

He bent forward and kissed her clit. She was surprised and then she was in ecstasy as he put his tongue and lips to work. Her first orgasm of the night was not long in coming though she had been desperate for it since the morning. As she climaxed, her fear, her shame and her doubt were washed away by its crashing wave. He didn't stop when she came. He kept at it and the waves seemed to only partially wash back before surging in again and again!

Kimberly had pleasured herself in the tub before, and even gone as far with a boy as to get fingered but she had never felt anything like this. It wasn't until the 4th climax that he came up. His face wet with her juices.

He pushed his left ring finger up into her and began to rub the front wall. His fingers were so thick and he was hitting spots she didn't know she had. While she writhed in pleasure, he used his right hand to wipe his face off with a hand towel.

With his finger in her and his open palm against her mound, he pushed her backwards until she was entirely on the bed then climbed up on his knees over her. He came up to her left with his finger still working. She climaxed once more when he brought his face down next to hers and began nibbling her ear.

With his right hand, he produced a blue vibrator. It was shaped like a silicone penis, almost as big as his but it had a nub with two prongs on one side. He moved it into position, as he slid his finger out, he replaced it immediately with the toy. She tensed and then relaxed in the sensation of it sliding into her. He locked his eyes with hers, a smile spread across his face, he raised his eyebrows.

<Buzzzzzz>

Kimberly had never played with toys like this. She was not prepared for the tingling surge from inside her and from the prongs against her clit as they came to life. She let out a loud cry of surprise and pleasure.

David moved the toy slightly, in and out, but never allowing it to break contact. She was cuming again as he worked. Before the last wave had washed away she surged once more. It was getting to be too much.

"My pants!" he gruffly said.

Kimberly fumbled with his belt but she couldn't focus. She felt like she was all thumbs. How could she think with the constant waves of ..... she fell back flat as she climaxed again.

"Naughty Puppy!" David admonished her. "If you can't use your hands, maybe I should tie them down and just fuck you like a whore!"

She rolled back up and grabbed at his belt again. He pressed the toy in deeper and pressed a button. The intensity increased. Kimberly clenched her teeth as she finally pulled the end of the belt free. She had the fly pulled apart. Oh God, she was so close! She had to hold back, just a little longer. Her fingers found his zipper and had it down. She was puffing air through her cheeks and squinting through the surging pleasure. He brought his knees together and she pushed his pants and underwear down to the bed.

His erect cock sprang up in front of her. Because it was what she had been doing since she arrived she opened her mouth and took it in. Then, with his swollen penis in her mouth, the taste of precum on her tongue, and the vibrator buried deep within her, she had a climax greater than what she thought was possible. She screamed into the head of his dick.

He put his free hand on her chest and pushed her onto her back.

"Now you're ready," he said.

He backed down, bringing his cock out of her mouth, pulled the vibrating toy out of her and climbed over her leg, pushing her knees apart with his own. He lowered himself, using his left hand to guide his member, still wet with her saliva to where it was pressing up against her. Then, with a thrust, she felt a brief sharp stab that was almost immediately overwhelmed with more pleasure. Where the toy had been cold and rigid, he was hot inside her. She felt him begin to rhythmically start thrusting and she cried out once more. She was no longer a virgin and she had never before felt this good. She climaxed. She didn't know how many times she had climaxed in the last few minutes, but she didn't care. She wrapped her arms around her master as he continued to thrust into her.

It was done, she was an owned Nexum girl and she had given her virginity to this man as her master. In that moment she was happy to accept her role as his owned submissive. He was on her, he was in her and he had complete power over her. She called him master in her mind and knew that was exactly how she should think of him. She belonged to him and she looked forward to serving him for the next three months.

His thrusting reached a feverish pace and he pushed deeper into her than he had up to that point. It was so deep that it hurt and she clenched her fists. Her master was so big. She felt him throb and a sudden wetness inside her as he tensed up and let out a growling moan. Her master had just filled her with his seed. She was grateful for the birth control injection the day before because she relished the sensation.

"Thank you Master," she whispered as he put his head down on her shoulder.

"Good Puppy!" he replied. He propped himself back up and kissed her on the lips. "Did you enjoy your first fucking?"

Kimberly nodded. "Yes Sir! I can't wait to do it again!"

David smiled. "You won't wait long." His face adopted a serious expression, "It didn't hurt, did it? I tried to make sure you were very wet before we started."

Kimberly stroked her master's hair. "Just a pinch, and when you go deep. My master's cock is so big."

David gave a devilish grin and thrust once more, but he was already going soft so it didn't hurt like earlier. "You are such a dirty puppy!" he said.

"Thank you Sir," Kimberly said.

David pulled out of her and covered her cunt with the hand towel immediately. "Go get cleaned up and undressed. You sleep in the nude."

Kimberly held the towel in place as she could feel his cum wanting to leak out of her. She climbed out of bed and went to the bathroom.

When she returned, David was only wearing boxer shorts. His back was covered in line-drawing tattoos, but Kimberly couldn't see what they were in the dim light. He was climbing between his covers but he pointed to the round dog bed in the corner. "Fuckpets are not allowed on the furniture without permission. You sleep there."

She nodded and obediently went to the bed. There was a single knit blanket folded on it, she curled up naked on the oversized round cushion and pulled the blanket over herself.

"Good night Puppy! Remember, breakfast and blowjob at 8! The alarm is already set!" David said before rolling over.

"Good night Master." Kimberly replied. She was asleep almost instantly.

The Fourth

"Big day today Puppy!" Master David announced as the alarm went off. Like every morning for the past month and a half, she was naked under her blanket. She rose up and stretched letting out a high pitched yelp.

She looked up at her master expectantly. She didn't dare ask any questions. For the past two weeks they were deep into petplay. Her collar was programmed with voice recognition. If it detected an English word in her voice, it would administer a shock. For the first couple days she hand made dozens of slips, but by now her silence was second nature. If she needed to communicate with Master she could bark, whine, or yip.

"Ruff?" she let out an inquisitive bark.

He rubbed her head. "It's the Fourth of July, Puppy! Remember I had you clean the whole house yesterday?" He paused and looked at her, waiting for confirmation.

"Rawwr" she let out a playful growl. She knew he enjoyed seeing her play the Fuckpet even more. As frustrating as not talking and crawling around like an animal had been, she found herself enjoying the silliness of the role play and she liked making him happy.

"There's gonna be a lot of guests today!" he said. "Until now, I have only shared you with one guest at a time. Well you are gonna be tired tonight."

She whimpered. Over the past weeks, David had been visited by old friends from out of town three times, each time he was happy to let them use her for the night. Only two took him up on the offer one requesting a blowjob and the other had been a gentle fuck, but she didn't know them part of her was grateful, because she was worried that word of how she spent her summer might get out, but strangers worried her. She trusted Master David, but who were they?

"Oh, I won't let them hurt you." He reassured her. "And your face will be covered so no one will know who you are."

She panted in agreement to the precautions.

"Good Puppy!" He stood up and brushed his hand across her cheek. "Go make breakfast! After we eat you can get into your special outfit!"

Kimberly crawled on hands and knees out of the bedroom and down the stairs. Part of the puppy game meant she was only allowed to stand when her duties required it. Even when she was on the ground floor and knew that David couldn't see her, she didn't stand until she reached the kitchen and began cooking.

She made an omelet for her master, and, like every morning, she gave him a blowjob while he ate. Once she had swallowed his cum, she was allowed to make some eggs for herself, which she ate out of a bowl with "Fuckpet" written across the side, on the floor without using her hands.

Once everything had been cleaned up and the dishwasher was running, she crawled back up stairs and into the guestroom, which had since become her wardrobe over the past five weeks.

So close to the ground, the first thing she saw as she crawled in was a pair of shiny blue thigh high heel boots in patent leather. Once in the room with the door closed, she saw, laid out on the bed, was a PVC underbust corset with alternating red and white panels. There were no panties.

She fastened the corset and began working the laces. It was not the first time Master had her wear one so she knew how to get it right. Once she had it pulled tightly round her middle, she tucked the ends of the laces back up and under the garment.

The boots had zippers up the whole length. Kimberly cursed herself for not putting them on before the corset, but she managed to hold her breath long enough to get them on.

There was a set of red white and blue ribbons on the vanity, so she used them to tie her hair back into a ponytail. If Master was going to make her service other men, she assumed that meant blowjobs.

Once she was satisfied with her appearance, she got back down on the floor and crawled back downstairs. As she came around the corner to the living room, Master applauded.

"You look fantastic Puppy!" he said. He came over

and clipped her leash onto her collar before leading her to his office.

Master David's office was just off the formal living room, which David had lined with bookshelves. David's desk was against one corner, where his computer and notes were kept.   In the adjacent corner was Kimmy's second bed. She spent many days curled up there while Master worked, waiting for him to summon her to get him a snack, or a drink, or give him some sexual release. Despite not having a blanket, Kimberly had come to enjoy naps while Master worked more than nights in her upstairs bed.

As she crawled into the office, she could see that Master's chair was missing and his computer was off. The futon was open and there was a fitted sheet covering it. There were two stacks of towels on the desk. Master clipped her leash to a hook on the wall. "While the party is going on, you will entertain guests in here so they can have some privacy." David explained.

"Wuff?" Kimberly replied.

David smiled. "Yes they will be arriving soon. It's an all day party."

Kimberly whimpered.

"It's just for today! A special occasion! If you are good, I'll save some fireworks for you to see tomorrow after they go home." David said as he unlocked a cabinet over his desk. "Now, your outfit needs a couple more items to be complete!" He pulled out a bundle of blue vinyl and leather, setting it on the desk.

Kimberly looked at the pile and let out another inquisitive, "YAP!"

"I promised we would hide your identity!" David said. "But I also want to make this more interesting." He held up a pair of blue leather mittens that had dangling straps. "Paws up!"

Kimberly sat back on her haunches and raised up her hands. David took off her wrist cuff and slid the first mitten on, it went up to her elbow. Kimberly realized that it was soft but rigid, it had no thumb and forced her fingers into a fist. Once he had fastened the straps down, she saw that her arm ended in a useless blue ball. She whimpered.

"It's just to try out! Something special for the guests!" he reassured her. He slid the other mitt on and began fastening it. When he had finished he pulled out his phone. He fiddled with it for a couple minutes and then held it up in front of her.

"I disabled the shocks for a moment." he explained. "Say lobster."

Kimberly hesitantly complied, "L-lobster."

David pressed a button. "Don't stutter this time please."

"Lobster!" Kimberly replied.

"Good!" David hit another button. "I turned the shocks back on, but lobster is your safe word! If you can't handle anything today, say lobster. It will shut everything down and alert me so I can stop whatever is happening."

Kimberly was grateful, "Thank—", the shock caught

her in the throat and she doubled over as she spasmed.

"I told you I turned them back on!"

"Woof! Woof!" Kimberly said in an annoyed reply. Then she got a hold of her annoyance and gave a satisfied pant to let Master know she was grateful.

"Good Puppy!" he patted her head. "Now the last touch, to cover your appearance."

He picked up a blue leather bondage hood. It had a wide opening for her mouth and two button holes for her nostrils to breathe through but no eye holes.

"Ready?"

"Arf?" she barked in reply, unsure.

"Let's go then," he pushed the hood over her face and everything went black. It took several minutes as he laced the back of the hood tightly behind her head, leaving a gap for her ponytail to come out of. He fastened a collar around her neck that held the hood flush along the bottom of her chin. She could hear the click of the leash as it was moved to the heavier collar. She was blind, exposed, unable to use her hands and chained to the wall. With nothing else to do, she knelt on the floor and waited for the party guests to arrive.

There was no way to keep track of time, so she had no way to know how long it was before she could hear voices as guests were greeted at the front door. Her pulse began to speed up as she could hear more and more arrive. She smelled something baking and the scent of coffee. Eventually the voices grew louder as David began to give his guests a tour of the house.

They were just outside the office in the living room.

"...turned it into a library! It's not like we need smoking rooms anymore." David said.

"Is that a first edition?" a voice asked.

"Good eye, author signed too! It's about seventy years old!" David boasted. Kimberly was curious now. She hadn't taken time to look at his library and clearly there were some gems in there.

The voices were getting louder.

"To the office!" David said as she heard the door swing open.

"DAVEY!" another man's voice in shock.

"Do you like her?" Master asked. "My Nexum girl, she is here for the summer."

"Who is she?" a woman asked.

"Nope!" said David. "I promised to keep her identity quiet. You can call her FuckPet or Puppy!"

The woman sighed, "FuckPet? Really?"

"Yes." David said. "She is available to any of my guests today, but the mask stays on and if she says 'lobster' you stop and leave the room immediately!"

"Lobster?" the first man asked.

"Unlikely to come up in conversation." David replied.

"That and she is not allowed to speak anyway."

"Uh huh," the man said.

"Let's move on to upstairs!" David announced.

"If you don't mind," the first man said.

"Glen you are a horndog!" the woman accused.

"I'll skip Fuckpet if you're offering Betty!" the man said.

"No," the woman said. "I'll let Davey's Puppy take the honors."

"Suit yourself," Glen said.

She heard the door close. A moment later a pair of hands came around her from behind and squeezed her tits. She heard a deep inhale of breath beside her ear. "Do you suck dick?"

Kimberly nodded her head.

She felt him come around her. Heard a zipper and then the creak of the futon. She felt a pull on her leash and she let herself be led as she crawled across the floor on her mitted hands and leather covered knees.

He gripped her head between his hands and guided her. She felt his cock brush her cheek so she opened her mouth and took it in.

After weeks of daily practice with her master, she noted that Glen was not nearly as big. She was able to take him to the base, plunging his tip down her throat with ease. She worked her tongue along the underside as she bobbed up and down. She was proud of how good she had gotten at blowjobs and was actually enjoying herself when she felt him begin to pulse earlier than she expected. She was prepared to swallow every drop but he pulled out and pushed her backwards as his hot cum splattered her chin, and onto her tits.

"Aww yeah!" he grunted as more splatters struck her chest. "Wear it BITCH!" he growled. He moved above her as his ejaculation turned to a trickle that he dribbled over her lips. He gave one last grunt and plopped back down onto the futon. "First marks of the party! You can wear that the rest of the night." he said.

Kimberly tried to wipe off, but the vinyl of the mitts just smeared the cum around her face. She sighed in resignation as she listened to Glen pull his pants back on while she felt the tightness as the cum dried. She heard the jingle of his belt. She whimpered at him, hoping he would wipe off her chin.

"Aww, poor puppy doesn't like cum all over her face?" he asked.

She whimpered again.

"Tough shit!" he said and she heard the door open. "All yours," he said.

Kimberly heard new footsteps enter the room.

"Aww shit! That bastard!" a new man's voice said.

A woman replied, "What? Oh, what a cumdumpster!"

Kimberly whimpered.

"Oh, listen to that," the woman said. "Just like a sad puppy! Help her!"

"Fine," the man said.

She heard the footsteps come closer and felt a towel wiped across her face. He held the back of her head still while he rubbed her mouth and the front of her mask clean.

"Better!" he said. "So, what did you have in mind?"

"Me?" the woman said. "You were the one who said we should check out David's fuckpet!"

"Yeah," he said. "But I didn't think you would say yes!"

"Really?" she asked.

"Well, there is a lot we don't know about each other." he seemed nervous.

"Mhmm," her voice was next to his now, just over Kimberly as she knelt on the floor. She felt a long finger nail trace her collarbone. "You don't know how I would use David's toy?" she said.

"Ooh!" he said in surprise. Kimberly heard his belt unfasten, the long fingernails were not on her anymore.

"Do I want to watch you fuck her?" she said in a low voice above her. Kimberly felt the man's pants brush her knee as they fell to the ground. "Do I want her to eat me out while you watch? Ooooh, looks like you like this plan." she continued. Kimberly felt a hand on the back of her head, the fingers laced around her ponytail. "Or should she suck your dick while I sit on your face?" The hand on Kimberly's head guided her forward and she felt a penis press against her lips. She opened up and took it in. Almost immediately, her head was pulled back and she heard a thump from the futon in front of her.

"Lay back and eat what I feed you!" the woman said in a commanding voice. Kimberly felt her leash pulled firmly and she crawled forward up onto the futon. She could feel the man's bare legs on either side of her as she crawled up. The woman's hands guided her mouth back to the man's cock and she got to work. She heard the rustle of cloth and then the woman said, "Head back, mouth open!"

Kimberly felt the weight on the futon shift as the

woman climbed up. She heard the man making slurping noises and the woman said, "Yes there, Jesus you found that fast! Oh baby! You may be worth keeping around!"

Kimberly continued to work the man's shaft and she felt it grow even harder between her lips while she heard the man licking away at his own task while the woman moaned in pleasure.

"Don't you dare cum before me!" the woman demanded. "Fuckpet, if you get him off too fast I will spank the shit out of you!"

Kimberly slowed down, she could already taste a dribble of precum from the tip of the shaft in her mouth. She lifted her mouth off and licked down the underside to his scrotum. Without the use of her hands, she could only nudge the penis with a latex encased balled fist to manage it.   She felt the futon moving rhythmically under her while she slowly enticed the man's cock with her lips. She stroked her tongue back up the underside, took the tip in her mouth only for a moment and then back down.

"YES!" the woman cried. She heard a smack above her. "YES YOU WORM! YES!!! PROVE YOU'RE NOT USELESS!!!" She heard another hollow smack, the woman was hitting the side of the man's chest. "THERE! OOOOOOOHHHH GOD! YES!!!!! HHHHUNGGGGGHHHHH!!!!!!"

The cock in Kimberly's mouth pushed up deeper into her throat as the man arched his back.

"GOOD BOY!" the woman cried out. "Now fuck the

bitch! Let me see you fuck her!"

Kimberly felt the weight on the futon shift again. Felt hands on her shoulders lifting her up and away from the cock in her mouth. She was pulled up on top of the man and then pushed to the side. She landed on the mattress and was rolled onto her back. The man was on top of her.

"Take her!" the woman cried to Kimberly's right. "Show me how you fuck when you don't give a shit about her feelings! GO!"

Kimberly felt him thrust roughly into her. It wasn't like when her master took her, he always started slow and sped up. This man seemed to want to split her in two. He pushed up into her so fast that it shocked her. She didn't think sex could still be shocking after so many times in the past month, but this was so different, so raw and so harsh. He was pumping his hips with a primal fury and in moments he stopped, plunged as deeply into her as he could and held there while she felt the rush of his semen expelled inside her. He grunted and kicked his feet then collapsed on top of her.

"Good boy! Did you like your treat?" the woman asked and Kimberly heard a loud smack. The force echoed down from his ass and into her as she was still impaled on his softening cock. "Tell me you liked it!" She repeated and there was another smack.

"What the fuck?" he asked in confusion.

"Tell your mistress that you liked your fuck-treat!" She demanded and smacked him again.

"What?"

"SAY IT!!!" <SMACK> <SMACK> <SMACK>

"Ow! Ow! Ok Ok!!! I liked my fuck-treat!" he cried out.

"Liked your fuck-treat, what?" she asked.

"Huh," he was confused.

"What do you call me?!" <SMACK>

"MISTRESS! I liked my fuck-treat MISTRESS!" he said.

To Kimberly's surprise, she could feel him getting hard again inside her already. He was enjoying this.

"Good boy!" the woman said. "Now we know where we stand, don't we, worm?" she said.

The man pushed himself up off Kimberly, pulling out of her. She felt a trickle of semen down her ass as he did so.

"Yes..Mistress," he said sheepishly.

Kimberly heard the slither of a belt and a slap. "Out there, we are just Ben and Cathy, like always. But in the bedroom. I am your Mistress and you are my worm, and I always cum first!" the woman hissed.

"Ok," the man said. "Ma'am."

"Good boy, get dressed." she said

"Yes, Mistress," he replied.

Kimberly felt a towel wiping off her pussy. "You did good Fuckpet," Cathy whispered into her ear. "I read in a book once that beginnings are a delicate time. You helped me get this relationship on the right track." She kissed Kimberly, her soft lips pressing into her's. Cathy's tongue pressed against her mouth and she opened it, welcoming the woman. They lingered together for a few moments and then Cathy pulled back with a wet slurp.

"Good girl," she said.

Kimberly was still laying on the bed and catching her breath in shock at what she had just been a part of. Her whole body tingled.

She heard the door open.

"Excuse us." Cathy said in feigned embarrassment.

"Cathy, uh..Ben," a man's voice said. Then the door closed again.

Kimberly was still laying on her back on the futon.

"Ooh, I kinda wanna take you like you are right there," he said. "Don't move, puppy, I'm coming."

She heard the rustle of clothing and then felt him climb on top of her. He was already breathing heavily as he moved into place between her legs. She felt his tip brush against the lips of her pussy and then....a spurt of warm cum landed on her belly.

"Ahh SHIT!" he exclaimed. "Shit, Shit!"

She could feel him slump and she patted his shoulder with a mitted hand in reassurance.

He was off her and sitting on the side of the futon. "Goddammit!" he just sat there for a long time. Someone tried the door knob. "Just a minute!" he called. "SHIT!" he whispered. "Just a minute, who the fuck says that during sex?" he sighed and got up. A moment later she felt him wiping his cum off her belly. "I'm sorry, well, I mean did you even want me to fuck you? Is sorry appropriate?"

Kimberly shrugged and let out a whimper.

"Yeah," he agreed. "All fucked up. I'm just glad you didn't see my face. Thank you." He opened the door.

"Jim," a woman's voice said.

"Uh, hi Kelly," the man said, sounding confused.

"Don't bother looking, it's just me." she said. "I guess my secret is out."

"I won't tell if you wont," Jim replied.

Kelly's voice grew a little more sultry, "It's not just girls, Jim. It's a shame you already had a turn or I'd ask you to join us."

Jim's voice cracked, "Uh.. I, uhh."

"You could watch," Kelly added.

Jim cleared his throat. "Have fun Kelly."

The door closed.

"I'll bet he is an excellent fuck!" Kelly said.

Kimberly realized she was talking to her. She let out a neutral, "Yip."

"Uh huh…" Kelly said. "Keep your secrets. Here."

Kimberly felt a straw on her lips and sucked. She had not realized how thirsty she was until the ice cold water washed down her throat. She took another mouthful and swished it around.

"Cum mouth," Kelly said. "Wash that out!"

Kimberly swallowed that mouthful and took another long pull before sitting back and letting out a grateful, "Woof!"

"I've done my time working the fuckroom at parties." Kelly said. "This was an old tradition back in my school days." She was moving around the room. "Before Nexum, the guys would pool their cash and then us girls would draw cards." She sat down next to Kimberly and started gently massaging her nipples. "High card got the cash."

she said. Her hand moved down Kimberly's belly and pushed between the lips of her pussy, brushing her clit gently and then pressing in at the perfect pressure. Kimberly gasped. "Low card fucked the rest!" she said.

She pushed Kimberly onto her back while her fingers slid up into her. "Ohhh, it's a spunky mess in here she said." Kimberly felt her move down and felt her tongue between her legs. The sensation was new and amazing. "Let's see what he tasted like!" Kelly said and Kimberly felt the woman's tongue part her labia. She was slurping and licking and Kimberly's knees bent while her toes tried to curl inside her boots. Kelly was licking her clit and Kimberly clenched her eyes shut as she let out a wordless wail of pleasure while she came.

Kelly was climbing up and kissed Kimberly on the mouth. Kelly's lips were wet and slick and had a tangy taste Kimberly remembered from when Master made her lick his cock clean after fucking her.

"You like the taste of your own pussy?" Kelly asked. Obediently, Kimberly nodded.

"Good!" Kelly said. "Try mine!" Kelly rolled off onto her back next to her and then pulled Kimberly on top of her. She pushed Kimberly's hooded head as she crawled down Kelly's body to between her legs.

She could feel the hairs of Kelly's bush between her lips as she probed with her tongue for Kelly's clit. The taste helped guide her and the hint of metallic tang told her she had found the spot.

Soon Kelly's thighs were up as her knees bent. Kimberly continued to copy the same actions Kelly had used and Kelly started to writhe on the mattress. At last, Kelly grabbed Kimberly's ponytail and held her face down in her crotch while she cried out. She didn't let Kimberly stop. She kept her down there for two more orgasms before pulling her leash and drawing her up to her mouth for a deep kiss.

Kelly gave Kimberly another drink of water, "Stay Hydrated," she said before she left, greeting Kimberly's next guest.

The party carried on and it seemed there was always someone waiting at the door when the last person left. Her jaw was getting tired from giving blowjobs and her thigh muscles were tight, she knew they would be sore tomorrow.

As the latest man wiped his cum off her ass, she contemplated calling "Lobster" out of pure exhaustion. She tried to tally up her day, how many blowjobs she had given, how many times she had been fucked but she had lost track at some point. The man finished cleaning her off and gave her a solid smack on her ass before walking out the door. She heard more movement before the door closed.

"Oh Dude!" A voice Kimberly recognized said. Kimberly's mind was suddenly racing and she propped herself up on her elbow listening. Where had she heard that voice before?

"I told you! Uncle David is a fucking legend!" Said another voice and, to Kimberly's horror, it clicked. Steve and Justin were two of the worst pigs in her entire high school. The girls who knew, called them "Pump n Dump" because of their reputation. They had left a trail of one night stands and humiliated ex girlfriends in their wake. By the end of senior year, they both were seeing girls from other schools because her class all knew better. Now they were in here with her.

"Think we know her?" Steve asked.

Kimberly heard a pair of shoes hit the floor. "Does it matter?" Justin asked. "She's free to use for the party so let's use her!"

"I call mouth!" Steve called out. "I want to fuck her face!"

Kimberly heard a zipper and the rustle of cloth.

"Fine by me," Justin replied. "Up on all fours bitch!" he commanded.

Kimberly rolled over and lifted herself up on the futon. She felt the mattress shift behind her and a hand on her ass. The mattress shifted in front of her too. She felt pressure against her labia and then felt Justin slide into her as Steve's cock pressed her lips. She opened her mouth and he pushed it into the back of her throat.

"Bet I can last longer!" Steve said above her.

"Fuck that! I'm trying to get off!" Justin replied and started rutting into her forcing her forward onto Steve's cock as he smacked her ass repeatedly. She wiggled her tongue against him and he began to thrust in and out of her mouth, hitting the back of her throat with each thrust, she fought hard to suppress the need to gag as she choked on his cock.

She opened her mouth and let the drool flooding her mouth drain out the sides as she tried to hum through the ordeal.

The result was a "gluck gluck gluck" sound as Steve thrust over and over again while at the same time she felt Justin ramming his cock into her almost without rhythm.

"Listen to her choke on it!" Steve boasted as she continued to take him in her mouth. She tried to pull back but Justin pushed into her from behind forcing her to remain in place while Steve smacked his belly into her forehead. She felt the mask growing wet as tears filled her eyes from the choking.

She felt Justin grow still and once again felt a man fill her with his seed. He pulled out of her and she felt his seed run down her thighs. She rocked backward and put a rounded mitt on Steve's hip to keep him back while she worked the tip of his shaft.

"Oh fuck! She knows what she's doing!" Steve exclaimed. "I'm going to blow like a fucking volcano!" He put his hands on Kimberly's shoulders and then grabbed her ponytail. "Oh SHIT!" he exclaimed.

His cock twitched in her mouth and then her tongue was bathed in bitter salty fluid. She took him in a little deeper, wanting to keep it off her face and she sucked as he ejaculated. She swallowed and continued sucking until the last drops had been pulled from him. She swallowed again and pulled away, sitting down on her knees in the damp spot under her.

"Holy shit!" Steve gasped.

"I bet I know who this is!" exclaimed Justin.

Kimberly's heart raced. She silently begged them to just leave!

"Wha?" said Steve, somewhat in a daze. "Dude, I haven't had my dick sucked like that since Lisa Kris junior year."

"Close!" Steve said. "But I saw Lisa at the pool a couple days ago. Word is she tried for a Nexum but didn't make the cut!"

Kimberly was surprised to hear this. This was all Lisa and Shauna's idea after all. Kimberly wondered if Lisa wasn't willing to budge on her limits. As she tried to coax more spit into her mouth to help her swallow down the taste of Steve's cum, she envied Lisa a little. The last hours had been far more than Kimberly had ever expected.

"Ok, well I knew this wasn't Lisa! Hair's wrong." Steve replied as he flicked Kimberly's ponytail.

"Not Shauna either," Justin added. "No spot on her ass."

"No shit, you fucked Shauna too?" Steve asked.

"Bro!" Justin exclaimed. "I was the one who told you to hit that!"

"Oh yeah!" Steve said. He lifted Kimberly's face by her chin. "So who?"

"You're not gonna believe who we just fucked!" Justin carried on.

The room seemed hotter. Please get this wrong! She couldn't bear the idea of everyone knowing she had spent her summer as a fuckpet. She chewed her lip but dared not make a sound.

"WHO?" Steve asked.

"So, I noticed that bitch April by herself last week buying coffee. So I asked how she was doing cause, you know." Justin said. "And she told me to fuck off."

"Bitch," Steve commiserated.

"So then I asked where her friend the Church girl was." Justin put his hand on Kimberly's shoulder. There was a pause.

"She said I'd never believe it!" Justin went on.

"NO SHIT!" Steve exclaimed. "Little Kimmy Masters, did I just cum in your mouth?!"

"...While I baked her a nice cream pie!" Justin patted Kimberly on the back.

This was too much. The boys were laughing and she imagined them telling everyone. She would never be able to face anyone ever again.

"Well," Steve said, "Let's see if you're right!" She felt his fingers fumbling at the latches for her mask. If they pulled it off they would know it was her. She didn't have any way out.

"LOBSTER!" she cried out.

"What the fuck?" Steve asked as he continued to pull at the straps.

"LOBSTER   LOBSTER   LOOOOBSTER!!!!!"   she screamed!

"Dude! STOP!" Justin demanded. "That's the safety word!"

"Fuck off!" Steve said. He had loosened the last strap.

"STOP! STOP STOP!" Kimberly pleaded.

"Sounds like Kimmy Masters," Steve said laughing.

"Dude STOP!" The mask pulled away in time to see Justin shoving Steve away. Kimberly threw her face down onto the mattress as the two boys wrestled off the futon and onto the floor.

The door burst open and David strode in.

"WHAT THE FUCK?" he shouted and he grabbed the boys by the back of the neck.

"AAAAAGGGHHH!!" they both exclaimed as he pulled them apart. He shoved Steve at the door and he slammed into the frame face first.

"Aww WHAT THE FUCK!" he exclaimed and then dodged out of the room as Justin was pushed after him.

"Wait here!" David said to Kimberly before storming out of the room, pulling the door shut behind him.

Kimberly sat there in stunned silence.

She had failed. Six weeks of sucking dick and getting fucked and she likely hadn't made enough to even make a dent in her education. She cursed to herself. Only half the time contracted, no completion bonus. As she waited, she did the math in her head, about 60 grand. It would pay for a few semesters, but forget grad school or any extras. Then she thought about what had just happened.

They knew her! Steve and Justin knew it was her. They had even pulled her mask off! By tomorrow everyone from Kimberly's school would know that she had whored herself out for the summer! She imagined arriving on campus and all the eyes that would be on her. She started to hyperventilate as tears streamed down her face.

She couldn't go in the city! She couldn't go to any of the schools where her friends were going! They would all know her as 'Kimberly the whore.' She was ruined!

Her heart was racing and she felt sick. The taste of Steve's cum was still lingering in her throat and she felt nauseous. She couldn't catch her breath. There didn't seem to be enough air in the room. She tried to grasp at her collar but the ball at the end of her arm only clumsily pawed at it. She was choking and crying! She couldn't see. A blurred shape came into the room and Kimberly squeezed her eyes shut ready to be used again.

"Hey! Hey hey… shhhh shhhh." David said to her in calming tones as shut the door and sat down beside her. He wrapped an arm around her and pulled her into his embrace. "It's over, Kimberly. It's ok."

"They knew!" she choked out between sobs. "They know it's me! They're gonna tell!" she managed to exclaim.

"No!" David said soothingly. "They're not going to say a thing."

"They will!" Kimberly said petulant! "It's what they do! Pump and Dump!" she added bitterly.

"Not this time." David said.

"It's what they do!" Kimberly said again. "You don't know them!"

"Oh, but I do." David said and patted her on the knee. "Justin is my nephew and I just had a very direct talk with them."

"You did?" Kimberly had caught her breath.

"Oh yes, and I can be very persuasive!" he said.

"What did you say?" Kimberly asked.

"I reminded him that his rich Uncle David was paying for his education. I went on to inform him that if word of Uncle David's Nexum contract got out in any way at all, he would be cut off and out of the will!" David chuckled.

"And Steve?" Kimberly asked.

"I listened to what they had to say, kicked the shit out of Steve, told him I'd kick the shit out of him again if he talked and then told Justin I'd cut him off if Steve talked too!" David's tone was not as calm as it had been a moment ago. Kimberly looked down at his hand on her knee. His knuckles were bleeding.

"Thank you!" she said. "If you take these mitts off, I can go get my own clothes on to wait for the car."

David took her left hand and began unfastening straps. "Are you ending your contract early? It's your right of course."

Kimberly looked up at him in confusion. "I said Lobster!" she said. "I thought that meant that I had terminated the contract!"

David pulled the mitt from her hand and started on her right hand. "Safety words stop play, they don't end dynamics." He shook his head. "When you said it, you just told me you needed a break for us to discuss what's not working for you. Do you want to leave?"

Kimberly took a deep breath. "No. I want to finish." she said.

David pulled the second mitt off her hand and kissed her gently on the forehead. "Tomorrow then," he said. "You're off for the rest of the night. Go upstairs, use the furniture, get some rest. When it gets dark we will set off fireworks out front. You can watch from the reading nook window. If you turn off the light, no one will see you. The guest rooms are already spoken for in case anyone drinks too much, but you can join me in my bed or sleep on your own tonight."

Kimberly smiled up at him. Between the bondage hood and her crying, she was sure she looked awful.

"You can stay in our room in the morning," he went on, "remain unseen until everyone has left."

"Thank you sir!" she quietly said.

"David," he corrected her. "For the rest of tonight."

"Thank you, David," she said.

"Good!" He stood up. "I'll make sure the path to the stairs is clear. Go get some rest!"

After the fireworks were over, the party seemed to break up. A couple cars pulled away down the long private lane away from David's property, but there were those that remained. From the upstairs window, Kimberly saw David sitting with a couple who seemed to be in their 30s as well as another man on the back deck drinking coffee and talking quietly.

Kimberly got out of her costume. She took a deep relieved breath as she opened the corset. She folded the items and set them in a neat pile on her doggy bed before taking a shower. Once she had the dried cum cleaned off her face, hair and thighs she felt much better. She took one more look at the remnants of the party on the back deck before climbing naked into David's king sized bed. It had been over a month since she had slept in an actual bed. The sheets felt like silk across her skin. She relished the initial cold shock and then settled into comfort as his down comforter weighed down on her bare breasts. She lay on her back and thought about what had happened.

David had protected her. For weeks, the man had insisted that she was nothing but a Fuckpet to him. Just a Nexum girl he was playing with. But, when she needed help, he was there! He was there, he saved her, and then he made sure no one would hurt her.

This confused her. He was just an owner! He spanked her, forbid her from talking, made her crawl around like an animal, used her as little more than a masturbatory aid! This was a man she needed to endure in order to secure her future, yet, when she thought of him, her heart fluttered. Could a Nexum girl fall for her owner?

Kimberly was awakened as David tried to crawl into bed without disturbing her. As he settled in on his back, she reached over to his crotch. She was surprised that he was wearing boxers. Since she started serving him, the man had always slept naked. She found the slit and slid her hand through it, wrapping her fingers around his cock.

"That's nice Puppy, but you have the night off," he

said.

Kimberly rolled over onto her side facing him. "What if this is what I want to do with my night off. Not as your Puppy, but as Kimmy?" she said as she tugged gently and rhythmically at his hardening penis.

David grinned. "It would be rude of me to give you a break and then tell you how to take it."

Kimberly grinned at him. She pulled her hand out from the slit in his boxers and pulled them down. He was already as hard as a rock standing at attention, pointing up at his belly. She climbed up over him and straddled him, using her right hand to glide the tip of his penis into her. She sighed as she slid down on him. She had never been on top before and his cock was hitting all new places inside her. She slid all the way down taking his long and thick member into her until she felt him pressing against her cervix. She rose back up while swaying her hips. He put his hands on either side of her hips. She slid down again and back up. She knew she wouldn't be able to cum from this position but it was so comforting having him inside her that she didn't want to get off. As good as it felt, this was going to be all for him. She began to slide up and down on him faster.

"Ohhh Kimmy!" he sighed. He moved his hands from her hips and reached up to cup her tits. She continued to bob and sway on him. Their breathing was heavy but in sync. She was loving the feeling of control she had on top. Suddenly his hands shot down from her tits back to her hips. He pulled her down onto him and cried out "OOOOOhhhhhhhhAAAAAA" while kicking one foot. After over a month of him fucking her, and getting his dick sucked, this was the first time Kimberly had made David scream.

She stopped her dance on him and slid down again. Everything was much wetter now. She could already feel him softening inside her. She looked down on him with a smile, and he looked up at her in surprise.

"Thank you for tonight, Master." she said. Then she climbed up off him and went into the bathroom to clean up.

Last Morning

The alarm started beeping. Kimberly lifted her head and began to swing her legs toward the edge when David's hand caught her upper arm.

"Not yet Puppy!" he said.

She rolled over to face him. She loved waking up beside her master and wanted to show him. She licked her lips and looked down. He raised his eyebrows and rolled onto his back.

She climbed between his legs and kissed his chin. She worked her way down him. Collarbone, right nipple, middle chest, top of the belly, bellybutton, abdomen. His cock was already hard, rising to meet her as she came down. She wrapped her lips around it and took it down to the base, allowing the head to push past the back of her throat. She came back up and licked the tip.

"Oh no!" he exclaimed. "Change of plans!" He grabbed her shoulders and pulled her back up on top of him.

She laughed as he rolled her over onto her back with him on top of her. He held her down with his left hand on her shoulder while he used his right hand to guide himself into her bare pussy. Master had said he liked it clean, so she had been epilating it for weeks.

Kimberly closed her eyes and smiled as she felt him enter her. She shifted her hips and lifted her legs up, wrapping them around his waist and pulling him down into her.

"Ohh, bad Puppy! Dirty Puppy!" David said to her and then thrust himself roughly into her.

Kimberly moaned. "I am a bad Puppy, Master! Puppy needs a good fucking, Master!"

"Don't top me Fuckpet!" he said in a playful tone as he thrust harder and faster.

"Fuck me, master!" she panted. She was already getting close.

His rhythm increased and his cock was pounding into her now. "I..TOLD..YOU..NOT..TO..TOP..ME!" he grunted with each thrust.

She rolled her eyes back as the orgasm washed over her. He kept pace while she came and then he froze, she felt herself be filled with his seed. She loved the sensation of being bred.

David leaned down and whispered in her ear. "Dirty Puppy's gonna wear her remote today."

"Yes, Master," she replied.

He kissed her and then climbed off, and headed for the bathroom.

Kimberly rolled off on her side. Her foot brushed the round dog bed as she stood. It had been a while since she had slept down there. Master had been inviting her into his bed so often that not being invited had become a form of punishment.

Half an hour later, Kimberly was plating her

master's sausage and eggs when she felt the vibrator she wore inside her come to life. She slammed her knees together and bent as she felt it climb in intensity and then fall. Looking behind her, she saw David holding his phone and grinning.

"Good Puppy! Just checking!" he said.

Kimberly grinned back at him before turning around to finish putting breakfast together. Two plates, with silverware.

They had been eating breakfast at the same time since right after the 4th of July, David would rest his hand on her ass while she ate from her bowl on the floor. Two times he dropped his pants to fuck her doggy style while telling her to keep eating. Both times he seemed unsatisfied with the experience. Kimberly guessed it didn't live up to how he imagined it. A couple days after the second time, Kimberly had her face buried in her bowl, grabbing pieces of waffle up when he said, "Come up here and eat with me Puppy."

Kimberly looked up at him and he was gesturing to the chair opposite his seat. Kimberly brought her bowl to the table and then put her face back into it. When she finished, she looked up and saw David looking at her while holding his phone.

"Use a plate and utensils at lunch and from there after," he said. "I'm going to turn off the speech restrictions at meals. It would be nice to have someone to talk to."

After that, Kimberly had been eating with her master. While they ate, David would ask about her. What she planned to study in college, what movies she liked, and where she hung out with her friends. When he asked about her upbringing, he immediately detected her hesitancy as she tried to talk about what had happened with her mother over the last year. "We can talk about something else," he interrupted. "Have you ever ridden a horse?"

She told him she never had and he immediately got to his feet. "Then we will have to fix that!" He then led her out to the barn for the first of many lessons. He never turned the speech restriction back on.

As Kimberly finished eating, she saw that David was finishing as well. She slid off her chair and onto all fours. "Is Master ready again?"

David grinned down at her. "You can try," he said as he pushed his chair back and turned it 90 degrees.

"I always get my cum," Kimberly replied as she crawled between his legs and opened his pants.

While she extracted his penis and began to suck on it while it hardened, David tapped his phone.

The surround sound speakers came alive with hard rock. The vibrator she had inserted was sync'd to his play list. Each drumbeat thumped through the toy in her pussy as she coaxed him into arousal again. Because they had just fucked upstairs less than an hour earlier, it took her a while to get him hard. Once he was up, she could taste drops of precum almost immediately. Those bitter drops were like a tease as she continued to suck and bob while he stroked her hair.

The 80s rock beat reached a boiling point and

Kimberly moaned into David's cock as she climaxed. On her knees, with her Master's cock in her mouth and an orgasm echoing through her body, she suddenly realized that she was happier here than she had been in years at home. Tomorrow, she was moving into her dorm, and she had to admit that she was sad to go.

David had been extremely helpful. As the summer progressed, David ensured that the money she was earning went into the account she had arranged with Mr. Darrow. With her blessing, Mr. Darrow then used that fund to handle her college registration fees, dorm payment and other necessities. When the driver from Mr. Darrow's office dropped her off for freshman orientation tomorrow, she would be paid through the semester! The only thing left for her would be buying her necessities from the spending fund that was set up. Her first nights would be sparse, only the furniture the campus provided and the clothes she had left with Mr. Darrow, but she could handle it. As she continued to work her tongue around the tip of David's penis, she tried to make a list of what she would need. Sheets, a computer, maybe a small TV and...

David switched the music again, this time, speed metal. Any hope of coherent thought left Kimberly as the vibrator inside her kicked into overdrive.

She began to just bob on his dick, deepthroating him each time in a kind of jackhammer to the music as she swayed her hips and shifted her body.

The movement pushed the inserted toy against new places and she nearly choked as the second orgasm seemed to rush in and wash over her. She didn't know if she was having a third or if the last one just kept going but she could feel it from her crotch up her back into her shoulders. She tensed and rose up on her knees. His cock was still pushed into her throat, she had forgotten she was sucking it for a moment. She slid back enough to let her whimper escape her throat. She was puffing past it. She couldn't get enough air.

His cock twitched and a sudden blast of salty fluid hit the back of her throat.

The music was relentlessly driving the toy on stronger and faster.

She was cumming again as his semen filled her mouth. She screamed and white cum dribbled from her chin. She felt warm fluid around her knees. She had squirted. She was a mess. She tried to lick off the cum that had dribbled down his dick. She sucked off what she could and then went down to lick the chair and his balls too but the music was still rolling and she seized, clenching her fists on his thighs as she came again.

"Too much!" she gasped.

David quickly tapped his phone. The vibrator continued. He cursed and picked his phone up. "Shit, it's locked!" He tapped out a code and then hit the phone again.

The music stopped. The vibrator went silent. Kimberly went down on her hands and knees looking at the puddle of fluid under her and the trail of cum on her tits and on the floor.

"I'm gonna miss our breakfasts, Puppy," David said.

"Me too Master," Kimberly panted between breaths. After she finished clearing up the dishes and mopping the floor she was surprised to see David leaning against the kitchen door jam watching her with a half smile. As soon as she saw him, his thumb moved on his phone and she bent over again when the vibrator slid to full intensity. She caught her breath and stood back up. The buzzing inside her was steady and frustrating but it wouldn't be enough to give her another climax alone as long as she kept her mind occupied.

"What would my Master like to do with his last day as my owner?" She asked as she grinned at him.

"Keep you occupied," he replied. His thumb moved and the vibration went from a steady strong rumble to a pattern of slowly rising intensity that dropped off suddenly only to start climbing again. Now Kimberly knew she couldn't cum even if she tried. The drop off was timed just where it needed to be. David seemed to sense the change in her expression and smiled.

"Occu-pied?" Kimberly stuttered as the toy hit another peak and dropped off.

"Well, that cunt of yours," he said. "It's going to have something in it all day." He walked over to Kimberly and put his hand behind her head, his other hand cupping her bare breast. "Every time I kiss you, I worry I won't be able to stop!" He whispered to her before he pulled her toward him. She lifted up on her tip-toes, closed her eyes and let herself be overwhelmed in his embrace as his tongue entered her mouth. He held her there, his left hand sliding down her side from her breast and then across to her crotch. She felt his fingers brush across her clit and then she felt pressure as he pulled the tail of the vibrator. She relaxed her pussy and the toy slid out of her, still buzzing through its pattern. He dropped it on the floor and she felt a twinge of annoyance as she had just mopped. His hand went to his pocket and then was cupping her pussy once more.

She felt something hard and round pressed up into her, followed by a second. They seemed to clack and shift on their own. Ben Wa Balls!

David pulled her head forward and whispered in her ear as he pushed the balls deeper inside her. "For today, this is still my pussy."

"Yes Master!" she agreed. Her entire body tingled when he talked to her like this.

"For the rest of the day, it will always have these balls, a vibrator, a dildo or me inside it!" he said. "Just something to remind you that it belongs to me!" He pushed the balls up one more time and then stepped back. "Go get dressed, let's have a trail ride." He turned and went towards the door. "I'll see you in the barn!"

Kimberly found an outfit laid out on the bed. Black lace thong. Black job-hoppers, black boots, and a black string bikini top. She grinned. David loved to see her skin. She pulled the outfit on. The leggings were skin tight, the boots came almost to her knees and the bikini cups sat on top of her tits rather than cupped them.

As she dressed, every move she made sent the balls whirling inside her, because she was clenching to hold them in place, it was impossible to ignore the sensation. While the vibrator had been much more intense, this was constant awareness.

When she had the outfit on, she tied her hair back into a ponytail using a black ribbon. Inspecting herself in the mirror, she added a white ribbon six inches lower creating a handle just in case her master wanted to pull her hair. She smiled at this as she remembered him pulling on her ponytail two nights ago while he had fucked her from behind on the bed. She shifted her hips as they tingled at the memory and the balls whirled inside her. She let out a satisfied sigh.

"You are one hot slut," she said to herself with a smile before heading to the barn.

David had already saddled the horses by the time she arrived. He was looking down at his watch while patting a crop against his thigh. "Looks like you made me wait five minutes, Puppy!"

Kimberly put on a fake pout, "Oh no! What will you do to me, Sir!" she said. She looked at the crop hungrily. Until this summer, she never would have believed how much she enjoyed the sting of a good whipping. She clenched her thighs together at the thought.

"I should give you two strokes for every minute!" he

said. "But it's your last day...."

"I deserve it, Sir!" she interrupted him. "I wasted your time, Sir!"

He arched his eyebrow and tilted his head. He looked up at the frame posts between two stalls and then down at her wrists. "If Puppy insists..." He pushed off the wall and grabbed the chain hanging from a loop at the top of one of the posts. He took her left hand and lifted it to meet the chain, clipping her wrist cuff to it. He did the same to her right leaving her on her tiptoes with her arms stretched in a Y between the posts.

He walked around behind her. She shivered in anticipation as she felt a pull at her back and her bikini top fell open dangling only by the loop at her neck. She felt his strong fingers grab the back of her pants and pull down. She was already breathing hard. She heard the dirt floor crunch as he set his feet and..

<SNAP!> She was pushed forward by the blow as the sting on her right ass-cheek echoed through her body, met by the sensation from the balls inside her being shaken.

"ONE!" she declared. The rule was that she always kept count since she had been allowed to talk again. Any time she lost count, they would start again.

<SNAP!> "TWO!!" The sting was in the exact same place and it now burned like a hot brand had been pressed into her ass.

<SNAP!> "THREE!!!" she yelped this time. How did he always hit the exact same spot?

<SNAP!>"FOUR!" she said with more calm. It was the left cheek this time.

<SNAP!> "Aaaahhh! FIVE!!" Again he was hitting the new spot exactly! She clenched her ass and her thighs. She had to focus on her pussy. The balls felt like they could slide right out. She was getting so turned on!

<SNAP!>.....She paused to gain composure "SIX!" she let out a puff of air. She didn't know she had been holding her breath.

She felt the leather thong of the crop on her shoulder, gently running down across her back. It was gone. She heard the dirt crunch and tried to look behind her. David was at the tool rack. He had hung the crop up and was pulling down a hand stitched leather flogger. Kimberly's heart raced. She loved the flogger. She quickly looked straight ahead and her eyes met those of Valjean, the gray pony David had taught her to ride on. She smiled at the horse who seemed concerned.

<Swish SMACK> Her smile was cut short as she felt a collection of stings across her shoulder blades while the flogger raked its thongs.

"SEVEN!" She said in ecstasy as she felt burning welts rising on her back.

<Swish SMACK!> "EIGHT!" The leather had whipped the back of her thighs below her ass.

<Swish SMACK Swish SMACK!> Two rapid burning licks across her shoulder blades again. "NINE and TEN!" She cried out. "Thank you Master!"

She felt his warm hand on her shoulder and then his

rough finger tracing the welts on her back. He left and came back a moment later. She heard a cap open and then felt him applying lotion to her welts. It was soothing and sweet of him. His tender massage is a perfect contrast to his cruel whipping. At that moment she never wanted to leave him.

Getting on the horse with the balls in was a bit challenging. She was sure they would pop out as she swung her leg over the saddle. Once on, she had to lean back with her hand down her pants to push them all the way back in. They made the ride an experience. David led them at a trot and every bounce was magnified by the counterweighted whirl of the balls. By the time they returned to the barn, the arousal was overwhelming and she desperately wanted her Master to fuck her.

Probably to tease her, David acted like he didn't see her squirming in the saddle as they rode back into the barn. "I think cold cuts would be a good lunch today." He said as he climbed off Javier. He came to the side of Valjean as Kimberly swung her leg over toward him. He gripped her hips and lowered her to the ground. She looked up at him and closed her eyes.

He left her standing there as he began pulling at the straps on Javier's tac. "Go and get lunch started, and I'll put them away," he said.

Kimberly thought she glimpsed a mischievous grin just before he turned back to the horse.

One of the best things about being allowed to eat at the table again was the luxury of holding a sandwich in her hands. When she was still serving as David's full time puppy-girl, sandwiches for him, meant the ingredients of a sandwich cut into small bite sized pieces to serve as her kibble. While David would receive lavish hoagies with a variety of meats layered with cheese, lettuce, tomato, and seasoned with mayonnaise, vinegar, oil and Italian herbs, Kimberly had to make sure her meal was accessible and didn't make a mess of her face. She quickly learned that she needed to leave the condiments off. Lettuce would hold up ok, and she had to dice her tomatoes. As Kimberly would set her bowl on the floor to start eating, her sandwich bore much more resemblance to a salad with diced up bits of meat and bread mixed in.

Now she smiled at the memory as she layered turkey slices onto white bread for herself. Master David's meal was already made, cut and plated. She enjoyed stacking the sandwich halves to give it a more vertical presentation. She spread mayonnaise, laid round slices of tomato on the meat, cut it diagonally and brought both plates to the table. The balls inside her continued to whirl and she could feel them sliding around, making her hyper aware of her own vagina while she poured fresh lemonade for the two of them. Lunch prepared, she sat at her place, put her palms on the table and waited for David. It took a few moments for the balls to stop shifting inside her after she sat.

She looked at the kitchen, realizing that this was the last lunch she would make in it. She would miss lunches with David. Even when she ate them on the floor, she felt like the center of his attention.

There were times she would finish eating and turn to face him, ready to please him if he desired. He would hold up a small candy and whistle. She would lift her hands off the floor and adopt a begging pose then let out a "Yip!"

He would then feed her the candy and call her a "Good girl."

Kimberly loved it when he called her a "Good girl."

Just the thought of his baritone voice saying those words sent tingles through her. She shifted her hips and the balls rolled once more. She glanced at the door. What was taking him so long? She wanted him here and now. She wanted him to enjoy his sandwich, she wanted to please him under this table. She needed him to call her a "Good girl" today because, tomorrow she was leaving.

"Oh my God, I have Stockholm syndrome!" she said out loud to herself. How else could she explain that this man who had used her, degraded her, whipped her, bound her and owned her for this whole summer was the man she felt so much attraction to. Either she was undergoing some typical trauma response, or, there was something wrong with her.

The front screen slammed and David strode in. "Valjean had something caught in his hoof," he explained. "Just a river rock from when we were down by the stream, but it was stubborn to pick-out. Sorry for keeping you waiting, Puppy." He came straight to her and gave her a long kiss before washing his hands and then taking his own seat. "Looks delicious, thank you!" he said.

David's demeanor had changed over the past few weeks. He was kissing her without initiating sex, saying "thank you" and at times, acting like a gentleman. He still demanded sexual gratification fairly frequently as was his right by the contract, but he was more tender about it.

Kimberly sat back and the welts on her ass and back reminded her that "tender" was a relative term. Then she thought about the lotion. He seemed to spend more time treating the marks from her whippings than he did making them these days. She liked the new routine.

She thought back on when it may have changed.

About a week after the 4th of July party, David's friend Bruce had stopped by. David had her dress in an open-cup crotchless teddy with a pleated see through miniskirt. She served the two men drinks and then took up her place kneeling by David's leg as they talked.

Bruce looked at Kimberly, "So, she's Nexum?" he asked.

"For the summer. My puppy is going to college in the fall." David patted Kimberly's head.

"Does she… uh…" Bruce seemed uncomfortable.

"She is under contract to do as I say," David said. "So, yes."

Bruce shifted in his seat. "I heard that you were sharing her at the party."

"That got out of hand." David said. He patted

Kimberly on the shoulder.

Bruce nodded. "A big party like that, I can imagine. But, in a one on one scenario….." He licked his lips, leering at Kimberly.

David seemed uncomfortable. "Uh, um…" he looked at Bruce for a moment. "Uh, I guess it would be less chaotic."

"David, do I need to ask?" Bruce said.

David sipped his drink. "Just what are you asking Bruce?" His voice had a little sharpness to it.

Bruce seemed to miss the tone, or ignore it. Kimberly couldn't tell. "I'm asking to use your Fuckpet for the night!"

"She sleeps with me, Bruce." David said. "It's a security thing!" Kimberly didn't know if David guessed that she felt safe in bed with him.

"Fine!" said Bruce. "Then what about a blow-job? I couldn't make the party so it's only fair, right?"

Silence hung in the room while the clock on the mantle clicked away the seconds.

"Buddy?" Bruce insisted.

David took a deep breath. "Ok, fine! Puppy go do it!" Bruce rose to his feet and began unbuckling his pants. "That's the David I know!"

As she crawled across the floor, David got up and walked out of the room saying he needed ice. Kimberly glanced over her shoulder briefly and saw that David's glass was still half full on the stand and had plenty of ice.

Kimberly rose up on her knees in front of Bruce. The man's cock seemed to have a slight curve to his right.

Kimberly thought about him jerking off so much he had bent it and suppressed a giggle with a slight smirk.

"Like what you see Bitch?" he said to her. He grabbed his own cock with his right hand and put his left on top of her head. He rubbed the cock across her face and she opened her mouth to take it in. He put his hands on either side of her head and held her still while he began thrusting with his hips, driving his cock hard against the back of her throat.

Not expecting the sudden push Kimberly gagged on his cock. She tried to pull back but his hands held her still. He kept thrusting. She tried to cry out but with the constant thrusting the noise she made was a "Gluck, Gluck, Gluck, Gluck."

She raised her hands up and flailed them helplessly. Bruce was letting out a satisfied sigh.

Kimberly's neck was throbbing, she felt drool running down her chin. He was holding her head so tight that it felt like he was crushing her head. His cock began to twitch.

"WHAT THE FUCK ARE YOU DOING?!" David cried out.

Bruce let go of Kimberly's head and she leaned back, getting the cock out of her mouth just as a spout of semen erupted from it and left a warm, wet line down her chin and neck. The second pulse caught her right eye and burned. She clenched her eyes shut and turned, feeling another spurt against her cheek and into her hair.

"DAMNI!" Bruce cried out. "You fuckin ruined the

moment Dave!"

Kimberly heard a rush of footsteps and a scuffle.

"What the fuck!" Bruce cried.

"Kimberly get on your feet and go to our room!" David demanded.

Kimberly tried to open her eyes but the right one burned. She wiped the cum away with her finger while walking out of the room looking out of her left eye. She never knew what happened, but she heard Bruce leave soon after.

David cleared his throat.

Kimberly had been lost in the memory.

"I asked if you weren't hungry." David said.

She looked at his plate, it was empty. She looked down at her own. She hadn't taken a bite yet. She picked up her sandwich and smiled. "Oh, sorry."

"What were you thinking about?" David asked her.

"You," she answered.

David tilted his head. "Really?"

She smiled. "I have my suspicions about you."

"What's that?" David asked.

"I suspect that you might actually care about me." she said.

David sat up straight. The expression was serious. "What makes you think that?" he asked.

Kimberly smiled. "I have my secrets."

David nodded. "We'll see how you feel at dinner. Until then, meet me in the bedroom after you clean up here."

Unlimited

When Kimberly reached the bedroom, David was wearing only his boxers, sitting in a wingback chair. The under the bed restraints were out, clips resting at the four corners of the bed. On the floor a leather harness was waiting, strapped around a massage wand.

Kimberly didn't need any instruction. She untied her bikini top and let it fall to the ground before getting out of her boots, jodhoppers and panties. She hooked her finger into the loop that dangled from her pussy.

"No!" David commanded. "Leave those in." He then motioned to the harness.

She stepped into it and pulled it up, buckling the belt around her waist causing the head of the wand to push up hard into her. She adjusted it to line up with her clit and looked at David who just nodded at the posts at the foot of the bed. From each post, about 5 feet off the ground, there was a hook with a chain hanging from it. Just like in the barn.

"Face me," David said and Kimberly turned her back to the bed.

David was standing over her. She could feel his breath as he loomed there. He clipped her wrists to the chain, leaving her in a T pose. Then he knelt in front of her. He forced her legs apart, causing her arms to angle up. He clipped her ankles to chains too, leaving Kimberly helplessly bound to the posts. David looked up at her, smiled, and pressed the button on the wand.

Kimberly gasped as it buzzed to life. He nuzzled her belly and then ran his lips and tongue up her as he stood, staying stooped to suckle her breast. The buzzing of the wand echoed into the balls, amplifying the sensation and she strained against her ankle restraints. After sucking her breast for a while, he continued up and nibbled her ear. Electric current felt like it flowed from her ear down her body to meet a matching charge coming from the wand and the balls inside her. She moaned.

"Today, is your reward, Puppy." he whispered in her ear. His hands gripping her ass. "Today you can cum without permission as much as you want." He parted her ass cheeks and squeezed before rubbing his hands up her sides to hook behind her back. "And today you are going to cum more than you ever thought possible!" He reached down between her legs and pressed the intensity button on the wand, its tone shifted and she gasped. Then he pressed it again. She cried out as the waves overwhelmed her.

Kimberly lost herself. Strapped to the posts with the wand humming away, David moved his hands and his mouth up and down her body. She had no idea how much time was passing. She was quivering in a dream state as wave after wave of orgasm washed over her drowning out everything else. At last her legs were weak, and the sensation was overwhelming.

"Turn it down!" she gasped. "I need a break!"

The heavy thrum turned into a gentle buzz but it did not stop and she was left on her tiptoes in continued stimulation while she caught her breath and finally opened her eyes. The light coming in through the windows had moved across the floor. Her body glistened with sweat and now she felt a slight chill as the air conditioner turned on.

David went down on his knees again. He unsnapped the wand from the harness and let it fall to the floor with a thud.

He moved the straps aside, licked his lips and kissed her pussy. His tongue gently moving up from her opening to her clit. He sucked and began to move his tongue up and down.

Kimberly's knees bent. She was dangling by her wrist cuffs and moaning. Where the wand had been hard, relentless and brutal, David's mouth was soft, gentle and teasing. He took his time, coaxing her closer and closer to climax. He brought his hands up and used his thumbs to part her labia and then penetrated her with his tongue, the tip just brushing the threshold, then back to the clit. He repeated this again, but when his tongue returned to her clit this time, two fingers entered her. In moments she was screaming in ecstasy!

David unclipped her ankles from their bonds, then stood and did the same for her wrists. She brought her hands down to his shoulders wanting to embrace him but he bent and put one arm under her knees and the other behind her back.

He lifted her off the floor as though she were nothing and carried her from the foot to the side of the bed.

"Let me please you now, Master." she pleaded. She was not used to so much attention focused on her.

He laid her on the bed and then fastened her wrists and ankles to the clips at the corners so that she was pinned down, spread eagle.

"One for me, and then more for you." he said as he dropped his boxers. His cock was rigid pointed at the ceiling. He climbed on top of her, lowered himself and entered her. He took a slow and measured rhythm.

She bit her lip, she was afraid of how much she enjoyed being filled by him.

He pushed in as deep as he could and held there. "Not yet," he whispered when she looked at him. "I don't want my time inside you to end yet."

After a pause, he began again and Kimberly climaxed once more. It wasn't shattering like with the wand, nor sensually explosive like with his mouth, this was deeper, fuller, she felt the orgasm radiate up through her, into her neck and shoulders and out through her fingertips and hair. "Oh fuck me!" she pleaded and was a direction, not an expression.

His pace increased and he was soon hammering into her. She came again but this was more primal and she half moaned half growled. As she clenched her muscles he grunted and she could feel herself filling with his wetness.

He looked down on her and stroked her hair. "I love fucking you, Puppy."

She was panting. "I love being fucked by you" she said.

He bent down and kissed her tenderly on the lips and she felt her heart flutter.

He took a deep breath and pulled out of her. Rather than climb off the bed though he grabbed a large pink dildo with a rabbit attachment and a white handle. He pushed it up inside her and quickly snapped the dangling straps of her harness around the base holding it in place. He pressed a button and she felt the dildo get longer then shorter, longer then shorter, as it mechanically began thrusting into her. A second button press and the round hole on the end of the rabbit that had fit over her clit began to flutter with sound waves.

"OH GOD!" she cried as the combined sensations of being fucked and having her clit vibrated at the same time immediately returned her to the inevitable slope toward another climax. She flexed her arms and they pulled against her restraints.

David pressed a button and the flutter on her clit became more like an air cannon.

She whimpered and pulled at her bonds once more. Then groaned through an orgasm.

"Too quick" David said and he lowered the intensity.

Kimberly looked at him in confusion and

desperation as she lay there helpless while the toy inside her forced her closer and closer to another. She came again.

"Good Puppy, just the right level I think!" He pointed at the in-house intercom. "I'm going to take care of some things but I'll hear you. If you get in trouble, you know what to say and I'll be back in less than a minute."

She nodded frantically.

David walked out of the room.

She climaxed alone and helpless.

Immobile, strapped to a bed, with a sextoy forcing her to orgasm again and again relentlessly, Kimberly lost her sense of time. She didn't know how long it had been since David left, she didn't know how many climaxes she had. She had to concentrate just to remember her name. She knew a single word could end this but she didn't want it to end. It felt so good and they were just far enough apart that she could appreciate each one. More importantly, her Master had wanted her there and she wanted to please him.

She was surprised when she realized that the house was in shadow. The sun was low in the western sky. How many hours had she been here? How long could she take this? She smelled something cooking.

David came back up with a grin on his face. "Having a good time, Puppy?"

At this point, after so many climaxes, her mind was consumed by sex. "Fuck me Sir! PLEASE!" She begged and then arched her back as another orgasm rolled through her.

He was quickly on top of her, pulling the toy off the harness, moving the straps aside and was inside her. The mere act of him penetrating her was enough to trigger another orgasm just on his first thrust. He returned to a measured pace and she shook her head, "No! Fast! Hard! Deep!" She bit her lip and looked at him sternly.

He began to jackhammer her, their bellies slapping together. She screamed as he fucked her and came again. He was right behind her and in moments he was laying, spent beside her pulling at the clips for her wrist while his semen trickled down her ass from her pussy and added to the growing wet spot under her.

"Last fuck." he said as he finished unclasping her bonds. "You finished your contract."

She pulled her knees up and looked at him.

"You still have me tonight," she said.

"I know, but," he seemed to be looking for words. Instead, he changed the subject. "You can take off the cuffs and collar now. There is a robe in the bathroom, or you can put on anything you like for dinner. He turned and left her alone in the room.

She looked at the empty doorway in disbelief. She turned her wrist over to get at the clasp and stopped. David can say what he liked, but he still owned her and she was going to finish her time, loyal to her Master.

Because it was a command, she collected a green silk

robe with black trim from the bathroom door. It was short, not even coming halfway down her thighs. She wore the robe, her collar and her cuffs as she went down to dinner.

The kitchen was empty. Kimberly saw a dim glow from the dining room. She followed through and found the table set with David's good china. There was a whole roast chicken in the middle of the setting, surrounded by a colorful variety of sides. The room was lit by candle light and cello music was playing on the household stereo.

As she entered, David pulled out the chair he was standing behind and gestured to it. Kimberly sat and he laid a napkin across her lap before carving and serving the chicken. Once both of them were seated he realized that Kimberly had not taken a bite. "You don't need to wait for me. As I said, you fulfilled your contract. You're a free woman."

"Not till Darrow's in the morning, Master." she replied. "You still own me till then."

David sipped his champagne, freeing Kimberly to start eating. "They say your generation lacks integrity. Clearly they were wrong."

"I am glad you are pleased, Sir." Kimberly said.

"But," he continued. "You are not very good at math."

"Sir?" Kimberly asked.

"You arrived here under contract in the evening, 90 days ago," he said. "So your contract was fulfilled at 7pm today."

"But I slept in the guest room the first night!" she

replied.

David nodded. "I gave you a cooling off period, yes. But that was mine to give, I was already paying for your time."

"Oh," she replied.

David sighed. "Anyway, I wanted to have dinner with Kimberly Masters on her last night before college, not with my Fuckpet."

"Is there a difference?" she asked.

"I like to think there is." he said. "Puppy does what she is told because she is being paid to. She spends her time with me because that's her job. Kimberly Masters can say and do what she wants, so any time I spend with her is because she wants to spend it with me."

"I see," Kimberly said.

"If you want to take your plate and go eat elsewhere you are free to do so. But if you wish to stay at the table with me, do so as Kimberly, please. Take off your collar and cuffs." David tilted his head waiting for her answer.

Kimberly reached up and, for the first time in months, unlatched her collar and cuffs.

Dinner was delicious and the conversation was surprisingly engaging. David asked Kimberly about her possible fields of study. Kimberly talked about the hidden history of women's influence on economic trends including her favorite theory of how British housewives caused the American Revolution.

David listened with rapt attention.

When the meal was finished, Kimberly, out of habit, got up to clear the table and David stopped her.

"Tonight you're my guest. The guest room is all made up for you including clothes for tomorrow and your things were delivered from Mr. Darrow's office today." he said. "Orientation is a big day, and you had quite a workout today, you should get some sleep."

Kimberly realized that she was exhausted. As David moved dishes into the kitchen, she watched him for a while before saying goodnight.

When she reached the guest room her suitcase was sitting on her bed. More importantly, hanging from the dresser was a black and yellow t-shirt with her University's logo on it beside a matching pair of leggings that also sported the logo. She put her hand to her mouth in surprise as her vision blurred with tears. She had done it! Full ride, paid for, she was going to college!

She pulled an oversized t-shirt from her suitcase to wear to bed, but she had grown so used to sleeping nude that she soon pulled it off.

She couldn't sleep. It was a strange bed and she was excited and the room was too quiet. She rolled over for what felt like the 100th time and looked at the clock. It was after midnight and they had an early meeting at Mr. Darrow's office in the morning. She knew what was wrong.

David's door was partially open. She pushed it the rest of the way as she came into his room. As she lifted the covers, he rolled toward her.

"Kimberly? What are you doing?" he asked.

She leaned in and kissed him. "I couldn't sleep in the guestroom. I'd rather be in here with you,."

David pulled her down to him and kissed her back.

After fucking every day for three months, they finally made love.

Kimberly sat with her black University leggings crossed, she had added a black and yellow plaid skirt to the outfit just for some flair.

David sat beside her, and kept glancing in her direction as Mr. Darrow arranged two sets of documents into manila folders. Finally he pushed them across.

"Mr. Zorn, in here is documentation of the complete contract, and a receipt for the funds disbursed to Miss Masters for services. Please sign where I have indicated to confirm that you have received these documents and that Miss Masters has fulfilled her contract."

David pulled his own pen from his sport coat pocket and signed.

Darrow turned to Kimberly.

"Miss Masters, here is a record of your contract as well as confirmation of payment to an account YOU control of all funds due including the completion bonus minus the money already allocated for tuition, board and books. Please sign where indicated to confirm this is as we agreed."

Kimberly took David's offered pen and signed.

"Congratulations Miss Masters, your Nexum

contract is complete. You are a free woman and quite a bit richer as well." Mr. Darrow said.

Kimberly took a deep breath. "I can't believe I did it!"

"I'm glad you did," David said.

She looked at him with a devilish glare, "Well I sucked your dick every day, of course you did!"

David coughed in embarrassment while Mr. Darrow cleared his throat.

"My driver can take you to campus, Miss Masters," Darrow said.

"Woah!" David broke in. "Why don't you let me take you."

Kimberly smiled at him and grabbed his hand. "I'd love that David." she said.

Parking on freshman orientation day in a downtown campus was not an easy task. Kimberly was glad she had so few possessions as she walked six blocks through an off-campus neighborhood from the parking spot they finally found with David carrying her suitcase. In the front of the high-rise dorm building, SUVs were triple parked as parents and students unloaded bags, boxes and milk crates filled with everything from stuffed animals to book cases. Seeing this, Kimberly worried about everything she would still need to furnish her dorm. When they reached the front door she expected to take her suitcase from David and go up alone but he surprised her.

"I paid for all your books, I want to make sure they were delivered." he said staunchly.

Kimberly smiled at him as she fished her student

ID out of the manilla envelope of documents that Darrow had given her and swiped it to get into the building.

She found her name on the chart and they took the elevator to the 5th floor.

The door to her room was open. It led into a shared common space between the bedrooms. Kimberly was shocked to find the common space fully furnished complete with a brand new couch, wingback chair, and a large flat screen TV already mounted to the wall.

"Looks like I lucked out with roommates!" Kimberly said to David as she looked around in with a beaming smile. There was already framed art hanging from the walls!

"I guess so," said David.

Kimberly saw her name written on a card stuck to the bedroom door to her left. "This is me!" she said with excitement and swung the door open, then froze.

It was all done!

The simple bed had been replaced with one that looked like a sleigh, her closet was open and filled with brand new clothes ranging from casual jeans all the way to a ball gown. On her desk, a top of the line laptop was sitting on a dock beside a wireless keyboard and mouse in front of a 32" high resolution curved monitor. Kimberly turned 360 degrees in shock.

David walked past her to the all natural wood bookcase beside her desk. He scrutinized the spine.

"I have a friend on the faculty, based on your class choices for the first semester, he was able to recommend the books you would need outside the text to be ready for your assignments. It looks like they are all here." he said. He turned and Kimberly was kissing him.

They embraced for a long time and she had tears in her eyes as she stepped back.

"Thank you." she said.

"I wanted you to hit the ground running!" he replied. "I think you're going to be amazing!"

"I think you already are." she replied and blushed at how corny it sounded.

David turned to go. "I better let you get settled in." he stopped and looked over at her. "But, this Saturday, do you want to get together? A uh… date, not business?"

Kimberly smiled. "Sure, as long as I still get to wear the cuffs."

###

The Nexum Universe

The Nexum Universe is only slightly darker than our own.
When sex work was legalized, Nexum was invented!
In Nexum contracts, "Talent" is sold to "Owners" for sexual gratification over a period of time.
Initially, Nexum was voluntary.
As Nexum gained popularity, however, compulsory Nexum terms replaced prison sentences with almost no rights granted to those sold.

Bound In Nexum

The First Nexum Contract ever signed.

Privilege Chained

Prom Queen Penny is sold into Lifetime Nexum after a drunk driving tragedy.

Rebecca's Surrender

Rebecca O'Neal is framed by a business rival and sold into a life of Nexum service

Katrina's Seduction

Katrina is serving her 10 year Nexum Term as Hotel entertainment

to its software! Can she escape the glitch and be free
again?

About The Author

Ray & Katie Oslow

Ray & Katie live something of a double life. On the surface, they appear to just be one more conventional couple, going about their lives in the suburbs of the American South. Behind closed doors, however, they have a passionate and imaginative love life.

Working as a Husband/Wife writing team allows them to explore the themes of dominance and submission from either side of the dynamic. The imagination they have shared with each other for years is now spilled out on the page for the benefit of the reader.

Ray & Katie enjoy writing fiction where the balance of power is dramatically uneven. Many of their stories take place in a slightly shifted version of our own world, where personal autonomy can be traded away, or taken by rule of law.

Dark Fantasy Media

Website:
https://www.darkfantasymedia.com/home

Twitter:
https://twitter.com/D_F_Media

Facebook :
https://www.facebook.com/groups/dfmedia

News Letter:
https://www.darkfantasymedia.com/newsletter